DIANE E. TATUM

Main Street Mysteries #3

Attic Visitations

By

Diane E. Tatum

Library of Congress Control Number
ISBN

1. Fiction/Christian/Suspense/ Mystery
2. Fiction/Christian/Romance
3. Cozy Mystery
4. Women sleuths
5. Cozy Mystery (book)

ISBN: 978-1-0881-6454-9

Reviews from Beta Readers:

I think you need to continue the series. … There are some other twists and turns that would make a good story. I enjoyed the story very much. It touched on some areas which a lot of

writers may shy away from. The holding off of sex until marriage is a hot topic.

You wrote romance without crossing the line into steamy trash. So much good stuff in the book. :)

God bless,
Donna McHugh

Blurb for Attic Visitations:

"A series of mean-spirited shenanigans are trying Dorie's patience. She and Ross are determined they won't cancel the wedding because of them! The suspense keeps you from putting the book down."

Kay Walker Cook
"Remember All His Benefits"

Dedicated to

Jesus Christ,

my husband Ken,

my family: Dan, Becca & Kellan; Brad, Julie, Ethan, Paul, & Jonathan,

my friends,

and my Page 26 Word Weavers group,
who have read the journeys of Ross, Dorie, and Riley
through three Main Street Mysteries, so far.

Though one may be overpowered, two can defend themselves. A cord of three strands is not quickly broken. Ecclesiastes 4:12 (NIV)

Don't let anyone look down on you because you are young, but set an example for the believers in speech, in conduct, in love, in faith and in purity. 1 Timothy 4:12 (NIV)

Marriage should be honored by all, and the marriage bed kept pure, for God will judge the adulterer and all the sexually immoral. Hebrews 13:4 (NIV).

Chapter 1

Coming home from St. Louis …

Dorie Hudson and Ross MacAvoy pulled into the townhouse complex in Daelin, Georgia, after their Thanksgiving road trip to St. Louis. Ross had met Dorie's parents and three big brothers, and even better, they had approved of Ross as Dorie's fiancé. Wedding plans could begin in earnest now. Dorie was relieved but exhausted.

Riley McDonough rushed out into the parking lot to greet them. Riley was Ross's lifelong best friend, the closest Ross had to family. He was also Chief of Police of Daelin PD.

Riley gave Dorie a friendly hug. "How'd it go?"

Ross hopped out of the blue SUV. "Good. They like me."

"There was never any doubt." Dorie smiled at the broad shouldered, red-bearded, sandy -haired man she loved. "I just wanted them in the loop."

"Great. Now you guys can get married, so Ross can stop sleeping on my couch." Riley gave Ross a manly hug. "Let me help with the luggage."

"How'd you do over Thanksgiving, you know,

without your mom?" Ross pulled his suitcase from the hatch. "What's the news about your twin Ryker and your dad?"

Riley shook his head. "Ryker took a plea deal for manslaughter and arson instead of murder. He's on his way to prison. Not sure about Lee Kerr. There's no statute of limitations for child support. I'm not holding my breath."

Ross walked over to Dorie at the driver's side door. "You'd best get back to our house in Helen. It's late. I don't want you having a problem in the dark on the road up the mountain. The dog probably needs to stretch her legs." He enfolded her in a hug.

Dorie melted in his embrace. "Sweetheart, you need to be there too. Wedding soon?"

"It can't come soon enough, Darling."

They kissed.

Dorie reluctantly released him. "Sleep well. I'll see you in the morning at Java Joint." She climbed into the SUV and started it up.

"Be safe." He reached in and touched her lips. "I love you."

She kissed his fingers. "I love you, too." She put the car in gear and headed out.

Dorie unlocked the Helen house and released Star, her greyhound, to run through the house to the back door. She dropped her suitcase, coat, and backpack in the foyer. Star doubled back sniffing the air. She ran up the stairs to the bedrooms then down through the downstairs rooms. She whined at the door to the garage.

"Hang on, girl, I'm coming." Dorie jogged

through the house after Star.

She opened the door to the garage, and Star bolted in, sniffing the stairs to the attic and roo-ing her high-pitched howl. The hairs on Dorie's arm stood on end. Had she left the light on in the attic? She opened the garage door to the backyard.

The security motion sensor lights were already on before Star entered the backyard. Dorie went out with her and checked that the gate was closed. Satisfied that Star was safe, she turned and went back into the house.

Her gaze fell on strange things in Ross's house.

The lights in the kitchen were on. A dirty plate and glass sat on the kitchen table. One of the cabinets was also open. Lights were on upstairs as well. Tension that had released during the visit to her parents returned in her neck and shoulders.

Dorie grabbed her backpack and Star's leash and quietly backed out of the house. She climbed into the SUV, then called 911. While she waited for the Helen PD to arrive, she wrangled Star out of the backyard on her leash and into the back of the SUV.

"I'm sorry, girl, I know it's been a long ride, but we both need to be safe."

Then she called Ross. "Someone's been in the house."

"What do you mean?"

Dorie felt every nerve on edge. "The dog went crazy following a scent throughout the house. Lights are on. Dirty dishes on the table. A cabinet's open. Someone's been in the house."

"I'm on my way. Sit tight in the car until the police arrive."

Dorie watched the windows for some sign that 'Goldilocks' was still there. Her imagination had kicked into high gear, and she could see pretty much whatever she wanted. Was someone in the bedroom? Was there movement in the attic?

When the policeman's flashlight beamed in the window, she shrieked.

"I'm sorry." She recovered herself and stepped out of the vehicle. "I'm on edge."

"It's okay, Miss Dorie. We've gotten used to being here at Ross's house for one thing or another. What's up tonight?" The officer took pencil and incident pad out to take notes. "Dispatch said it was an intruder alert. Have you been in the house?"

"Yes, I took in my suitcase and my dog. She went wild chasing a scent throughout the house. When I let her out through the garage, I noticed the lights were on in the attic. There were dirty dishes in the kitchen." Dorie shivered, though it wasn't very cold. "Things were happening before we went to St. Louis. I thought it was my imagination with what was going on with Captain McDonough."

"You cleaned before you left then?"

"Well, no, not really. But I did put all the dishes away and turned off all the lights." A sense of being patronized seized her. "It is not my imagination."

"No one's saying that, ma'am. Just establishing the facts. Anyone else have a key?"

"Ross says no." As she spoke, Ross arrived in his grandpa's old truck. "Here he is now."

Ross joined her and the officer in the front yard. He wrapped an arm around Dorie. "What's happening?"

"Nothing. He's just asking insulting questions." Dorie moved into his warmth and sulked.

The officer offered his hand, and Ross shook it.

"How's it going, Bobby?"

"New baby. No one's sleeping. That's about it." The officer grinned back at Ross.

Typical Ross. He knew pretty much everyone in Helen and Daelin. She'd only been there six months. It had become annoying to be the only one outside the loop.

"You stay here, Miss Dorie. Ross and I will check out the house." The officer was already walking away from her as he finished speaking.

Star began barking. Dorie got back into the SUV with her. "It's okay, baby, I'm here." Her greyhound's head appeared over Dorie's shoulder. She petted Star's velvety fur as the men checked out the house. Star began to tick, a greyhound equivalent to a purr. She nuzzled Dorie's hair. Dorie wiped away anxious tears in frustration.

Finally, the men returned to the car. Dorie stepped out to hear their assessment.

"Well, Miss Dorie, I see the plate and cup. Are you sure you didn't forget to put them in the dishwasher before you left?"

Dorie huffed. "No, sir. I didn't leave dishes on the table."

"Okay. We'll see if we can get any prints off them." Bobby sealed a Ziplock bag, probably from her own kitchen, with the plate and glass in it. "We also found this jacket button near the garage back door. Is it yours?"

Dorie looked at another Ziplock bag with a large

5

coat button. She felt up around her collar of her coat for the button that held the strap around the neck. It was still firmly attached. "It's not mine."

"Maybe it's been there for a little while, and you don't remember. We'll see if any prints show up on it."

"What about the light switches?" The knot in Dorie's chest tightened. "Aren't you going to fingerprint them?"

"When did you last wipe down your light switches, ma'am?" The officer, Bobby, gave her a sideways look.

"Never. I've only lived here three months."

"Exactly. Unlikely we'll get any kind of print that matters on them."

Ross stepped toward her and gathered her to him. "Relax, sweetheart. It's okay. No one is here now."

"And he thinks I'm a lousy housekeeper and a liar with memory problems."

"No, ma'am. I don't think nothing like that. I just know that after a long trip, people are afraid to find their house not right. Sometimes people are just tired. Y'know?"

"I can stay the night on the couch if it would make you feel better." Ross squeezed her closer. "Would that help?"

Dorie looked from Ross to the police officer. "Fine."

"Good. I'll be going then." Bobby slammed his incident book closed. "Y'all try to get some sleep." Then he winked at Ross. "If you can, that is." He walked to the squad car and drove away.

Dorie pulled away from Ross and hit him in the arm. "You let him be condescending, sexist, and imply you were going to take advantage of the situation. How could you?"

She reached into the SUV and grabbed Star's leash. Star bounded out and danced around them. Dorie stalked toward the gate and let Star off her leash to run the backyard. Security lights came on as Star ran past them.

***

Dorie went into the house while Ross began emptying the car of Star's crate and essentials. He also grabbed Dorie's bag that she'd left in the front seat. He loved her, but she did not like men to treat her like a silly woman. Of course, he knew she was pretty much brilliant as well as beautiful. But she was a spitfire when men underestimated her. Ross knew better than that.

Guess it was another night on the futon. Was that better than the couch at Riley's? Of course, it was. He'd be in his own house with his forever love upstairs. Once they were married, he wasn't sleeping on that futon ever again. He needed to dump it since they had bought a new couch.

Chapter 2

Four weeks to plan a wedding ...

Dorie fumed as she lay under blankets and quilts. The late November wind whistled around the eaves and made her shiver. It wasn't as cold as St. Louis, though. She wasn't imagining things. This wasn't the first time she'd had things moved or heard sounds in the attic. Ross claimed no one had a key besides the two of them. Maybe they needed to get the locks changed anyway.

A thump in the attic made Dorie sit straight up. She listened carefully. She heard Ross downstairs, setting up the futon. Maybe she was just tired or over-imaginative. After all she was a writer. Her story on Ryker Johnson had won her attention and glowing reviews. Dorie was glad he'd pleaded guilty and was already in prison, hopefully for a long time.

Dorie must have finally drifted off to sleep. She woke to the smell of coffee from their fancy coffeemaker. Ross must have made a pot from the roasted coffee beans they'd picked up in a small specialty shop in downtown St. Louis. Heavenly. She stretched and jumped out of the cherry sleigh bed. She pulled on her sweats, drug a brush through her unruly auburn tresses, then raced downstairs for a cup. And Ross.

"So, there you are. I thought I'd have to send Star in to wake you." Ross corralled her about the waist and gave her a kiss to remember. "You look beautiful."

"Right. I've seen myself in the mirror this morning. Sweats and crazy hair do not equal beautiful." Dorie hugged him all the same.

"Darling, you are in our house, in my arms. You are beautiful and mine." He hugged her tighter and kissed her neck.

"Stop, your beard tickles. I know you somehow lost your razor while in California planting replacement trees, but it's not really necessary for our wedding, is it?"

Ross released a hand to stroke his coppery beard. "You don't like it? You never said anything about it since I've been back."

Dorie untangled from him and poured a cup of coffee. "I like it. It's very rugged and handsome. I just wonder if it's necessary in a tuxedo."

"Bet it would look good with a Ross kilt and tartan. I think my dad's is in the attic."

"Um, not sure about that."

Ross smiled. "What if I trimmed it back? Would that work?"

Dorie puzzled on that. "Maybe. Try it and we'll see. If we're doing a Christmas wedding, we need to get on the ball."

"I can check on the church while you're at work. What if the church is booked?" Ross poured a second cup. "The police station seems to be the place we spend the most time."

"No. Absolutely, no. Only if you're in the cells for some reason would I consent to such a thing."

Ross leaned against the counter. He looked so handsome in his red and green plaid flannel shirt and jeans. The hard labor he'd put in at the National Forests in California had broadened his shoulders and slimmed his waist. She had no trouble imagining him in a tux for their wedding, beard or no. A kilt? That she'd have to think about.

"City hall seems kind of sterile, don't you think?" Ross sipped his coffee. "Not sure where else to think."

"What about that antebellum bed and breakfast in Helen? I bet they have a grand staircase the bride could descend."

Ross began to snicker while trying not to laugh outright. "The Doll House? Dorie, you are not the most graceful person I know. You're the one who tripped into a decomposing body in the kudzu. Descending a grand staircase in a long white dress might be stretching your abilities." He couldn't hold it back, the laughter won. "I'm sorry but seeing you fall down the stairs in an elegant white dress ... well, it just seems like inviting disaster."

"What if I'm barefoot?" Dorie approached him. "Do I have a better chance of making it down the stairs and getting your attention then?" She put both hands on his chest.

"No fair." Ross stood and headed for the new kitchen table. "You know I'm having a hard time resisting my human nature. Don't start tempting me more."

Dorie knew she'd crossed a line. She did so love him. Her desire for him was tempered by their relationship in Christ. They'd wait until their wedding night. But he was always teasing her.

"Sorry. I'm human too, you know." Dorie sat down beside him with her cup of coffee.

Ross took her hand. "I know. Is former Mayor Goldstein's house still empty on the hills above Daelin? As I recall, it's pretty nice."

Dorie shivered. What she'd gone through with Hilde and the mayor seemed more than she could overcome for her wedding day. Hilde had an affair with the mayor, murdered her rival, and then tried to kill Dorie as well for figuring it out. "I don't think so, Ross." She checked the clock. "Look at the time. I'd best get ready if I'm going to make it to Daelin in time."

She jumped up, but Ross was faster.

"Wait. I know we are anxious for this wedding to happen, ahem, for many reasons. I'd be worried if we weren't attracted to each other. I'm glad to know that you are feeling the same things I am." He grabbed her hands, held them tight, and pulled her to him. "I love you."

Dorie leaned on him. "I love you too."

They kissed, then she ran upstairs to get ready for work.

***

Ross watched her ascend the stairs then sighed. Star nuzzled up to his side.

"Good girl. I love you too." She nuzzled him again, harder this time. He moved toward the garage door to let her out, and she bounded around him as he moved.

Star ran out into the garage when he opened the door. Then she stood at the bottom of the steps to the attic and whined. The door was open, and the light was on.

Ross opened the door to the back, and Star ran out onto the frosty fenced lawn.

He looked up the stairs, then took them two at a time. Was there something to what Dorie was hearing and seeing? Surely not. Ross reached the second landing and went into the attic. Everything seemed okay. He walked among the generations of junk, looking here and there. How could anyone ever tell if something was out of place? He picked up a few things and placed them on a shelf. He looked out the dormer window onto the foggy land. Is someone using the attic as a refuge?

"Ross? Are you in the attic?"

"It's okay, love. I'm up here, looking around." Ross was surprised she heard him. Dorie was extremely sensitive about sounds in the attic. What was she hearing? What was going on?

Chapter 3

Work and wedding plans …

Dorie pulled the blue SUV into her regular spot in front of the Daelin Beacon.

"Newsies! Conference room. Now!" Ethan Andrews, editor, called out to the newsroom. "Let's find a way to put together a paper this week."

Dorie dumped her things at her desk, grabbed a legal pad and pencil, and hurried to the conference room. She ran in and snagged her regular chair. The murmur around the table ceased as Mr. Andrews entered the room.

"Hope you've had enough holiday to last you until Christmas. We've got four editions between now and then. What have we got going?"

Reporters shouted out the stories they had underway. Dorie sat quietly while they all had their say.

"Oh, Dorie, I hear wedding plans are starting. Tell me all the details. My readers want to know it all!" Marie worked the local 'news'. As in community gossip. "Greg's already sent me the pic of you and Ross in the newsroom to run with it." She slid a print across the table.

Greg had captured the moment, that much was true. She had jumped into his arms, and he had kissed her. The picture showed her and Ross, very much in love, right after that kiss. While it made her blush, it was a very good picture of them. A great engagement-type picture.

"Great picture, Greg." Dorie spoke softly. "Thanks."

Greg nodded with a growing smile. "I thought this was the best of them. You can choose from the rest if you'd like."

"Save me a time to get all the details." Marie could be pushy and was not really Dorie's friend. She could be trusted to get her articles right, though.

"Sure. We don't know much yet. We've only agreed that the wedding will be Christmas." Dorie's information was met with whistles and catcalls.

"This year?" Marie's face nearly looked like Munch's The Scream painting. "How will you ever get it all done by then, much less work as well? You should give at least a year to get your dress and venue and caterer."

Dorie felt a resurgence of heat into her neck and face. She jumped up and headed for the bathroom to splash water in her face. She dried her face then looked into the mirror. Face, red. Hair, tangled auburn ringlets. Dress jeans and long sleeve tee shirt. She didn't really look like anyone's bride. Aw, Ross, what are we doing? We really don't know how to throw a wedding. Eloping sounds better and better. She put her face in the damp towels in her hands, hoping the feverish flush would subside. One of the side effects of having any red hair and a fair complexion – flaming blushes.

Marie poked her head into the bathroom. "Are you okay? I wasn't trying to embarrass or upset you. I was just surprised."

"It's okay. We just got home last night from St. Louis and decided on a Christmas wedding. We literally don't know anything else about it. Maybe we should just elope."

Marie leaned against the counter. "And not give Daelin a chance to celebrate one of their favorite sons and their celebrity reporter? That would be more upsetting for the town." Marie rubbed her back. "I can help you. I was headed to Atlanta this weekend. The 'Say Yes to the Dress, Atlanta' bridal shop is selling their last year samples. You don't seem to be a fashionista. You might find something amazing at a reduced price perhaps without any altering."

Dorie wasn't sure whether to be grateful or insulted. Was she a bargain basement bride? Did she want a gown that had been tried on over and over for a year or so? Would it need to be dry-cleaned first before she could even wear it? Her head was spinning, and a headache was on the horizon.

"What do you think? Do you want to make a run to Atlanta Saturday? I'll get you an early appointment so you can have the most choices."

"Will they even have appointments?" Dorie wasn't sure, but maybe it was the best way.

"Darling, for me you can have a private showing. Just give me your size and measurements and basic idea, and they'll pull all the dresses you'd like to see before the crowd gets in." Marie took that as assent, snapped her fingers, and marched out of the bathroom, triumphant.

Dorie looked into the mirror. Her face looked less splotchy. "What have I done?"

When she reached her desk, her phone was ringing the "Morning Coffee Jazz."

"Hey, Ross."

"Sweet lady, good day so far?"

"Marie wants to take me to the famous bridal shop in Atlanta Saturday for their sample bridal gown sale. She doesn't think we can put together a wedding in four weeks." Dorie was frustrated more than upset. How dare she!

"Sounds good. I'd marry you in jeans just as well, love."

Dorie picked up her coat and walked out the door to the sidewalk to have a semi-private conversation. The wind was strong and cold.

"Brrr!" Dorie shivered. "You are wearing a tux. Neither of us will be in jeans. I'll wear a dress of some kind."

"Yes, ma'am. Thought you'd like to know that I have reserved The Doll House Bed and Breakfast in Helen that you like for a Christmas Eve wedding and room and breakfast on Christmas morning." Ross sounded proud of himself. "You just tell Marie that."

"Is it big enough?" Dorie wasn't sure how big it should be. How many people is a small wedding? "Never mind, I have no idea how big is big enough."

"Don't worry about anything. Melody's Diner and Jenny at the B&B are coordinating food for a reception. Heather at the bakery will do a cake. I can get Riley and myself to a tux shop. What else do we need?"

"Invitations? A maid of honor? Flowers?"

"I'll head down to Marjorie's Flowers now, but I think you need to pick flowers. Jared can print invitations. We can talk about that tonight. We'll need a guest list, too."

Dorie turned the corner into the alley to escape the wind. "You seem to have this all in hand."

"You know, I think there's a bridal veil in the attic. I'll look for it and see if we need to clean it somehow."

Dorie laughed. "You never cease to amaze me."

"I have ulterior motives." Dorie could picture his eyebrows dancing up and down like Snidely Whiplash. "I can't take a chance on someone else whisking you away from me."

"Aw, darling Ross. Just won't happen. I need to get in from the cold. I think it's snowing." Dorie hurried back into the Beacon offices. "Lunch?"

"I'll be at Java Joint by noon. I love you."

"Love you too." Dorie returned to her desk and took off her coat.

***

Ross left the B&B and headed into Daelin. He drove to the downtown area and parked in front of the formal dress shop which rented tuxedos. Maybe he should wait for Dorie to look at the books. But it couldn't hurt to take a look. Marjorie's Flowers was just next door.

An hour later, he was befuddled. Who knew there were so many colors and styles of tuxedos? Dorie would need to weigh in on this decision. At least they had his measurements, and they would call in Riley to do the same. Flowers were also her thing.

Snow flurries teased him, one here, one there. Christmas was coming. The birth of Christ. The birth of their marriage. What could be better? Nothing could ruin Christmas this year.

"Sir? Can you spare some change?"

The lady was wrapped in hiking jacket and boots with a fancy backpack. Her straggly hair blew in the breeze. Probably homeless, he guessed. He opened his wallet and handed her a ten-dollar bill.

Ross popped into Java Joint. Angela waved at him with her neon green cast. Surely, she'd have that off soon. She was on the phone, so Ross walked back to Dorie's booth. She'd essentially commandeered the back-corner booth for her extra-work hours. The Wi-Fi and coffee made an unbeatable combination. Pastries and chicken salad croissants were also good there.

"Here ya go, Ross. Dorie meeting you soon?"

Ross handed her the cost of his special coffee. "Shortly."

"Pastry?" Angela waivered waiting for his answer.

"Sure, but I just was measured for a tuxedo, so I can't splurge much before Christmas Eve."

"Christmas Eve!" Angela's shriek brought the attention of the entire coffee house on Ross. "The wedding's Christmas Eve?"

Ross hated that much attention. He was a quiet guy. Dorie had pulled him out of his shell, some. "Calm down. Yes, we have a venue. The church was unavailable with so little time until then."

Angela sat in the booth with him. "Tell me everything."

Ross pulled out the pamphlet from The Doll House B&B. The register bell dinged.

"Don't you go anywhere, I'll be right back." Angela rushed to answer the bell.

Ross opened the pamphlet. The grand staircase twisted and turned in great squares. He could see Dorie on those steps, coming toward him in a white dress. Barefoot would be better. She'd be less likely to trip and fall without some fancy high heels. He smiled to himself. Regardless, he'd be at the base of those stairs to catch her if necessary.

DIANE E. TATUM

Chapter 4

Mysterious happenings abound …

Y ou're early." Dorie slid into the booth. "Are you okay, Ross? You look like you're in a faraway place and time."

Ross sighed. "Just thinking about our wedding." He handed her the B&B pamphlet. "There's your grand staircase, my love."

Dorie smiled. "Perfect. Definitely barefoot, right?"

"Please. I'd like not to call an ambulance before we're even married."

Angela arrived with a pastry for Ross, a double shot mocha for Dorie, and two chicken salad croissants. "On the house. Can't hear about the wedding now. Tell me later." Angela rushed off to serve her other lunch patrons.

Dorie laughed. "Matron of honor?"

Ross nodded. "Probably. She's the only one in town who knows us and delivers our perfect cups of coffee."

"Thank you for the bouquet of flowers. They're beautiful."

"I didn't send you flowers." Ross frowned. "I'm

sure I should have while I was at the florist looking at wedding arrangements and such." He pulled out his wallet. "Great, my credit card is gone. I must have dropped it when I gave the homeless lady a ten."

Dorie didn't understand. "Why would a homeless lady send flowers to me with the card signed 'Love Ross'." She pulled the card from the arrangement from her bag and handed it to him. "I'm confused."

"Me too. I better cancel that card and get a new one. Excuse me." Ross got out his phone and headed to a quiet corner to make his call.

Who would send her flowers? Maybe Riley, but he certainly wouldn't put Ross's name on them. Her brothers, playing a prank? Nah, they're too cheap for that. She really couldn't think of anyone who would go to that much trouble for a prank.

Ross returned to the table. "So, the floral arrangement was charged on my missing card at Marjorie's Flowers. It's been used at the grocery and the thrift shop since then. It sounds like the homeless lady."

"What did you do?" Dorie wasn't sure if she should be frightened or relieved. Knowing someone had done it but not knowing why was creepy.

"Canceled the card and the charges, except for the flowers. Called Riley to look for the lady. She needs help at the very least."

"Thank you for the flowers. You have such a kind heart, even if you are a little gruff sometimes." She took Ross's hand. "She must be cold and alone."

"Neither of us will be alone anymore." Ross stated the words, but ferocity stood behind them. He kissed her hand.

***

Once they'd finished eating, Dorie headed to Marjorie's Flowers while Ross headed to Daelin PD to see Riley.

The bells tinkled as she opened the door. A spry white-haired lady with a pixie haircut popped out of the back room.

"Miss Dorie! Soon to be Mrs. Dorie, I hear." She came out from behind the counter and hugged her because this is the 'hug your neck' South, after all. "What can I do? Ross was in earlier looking at flower catalogs, but he was just overwhelmed."

"No doubt, Ms. Marjorie. I'll be in later when I have more time to look. Today I want to know about this flower delivery to me this morning." Dorie handed her the card from the arrangement she'd received in the newsroom. "Ross says he didn't send it, but it was charged to his credit card, which went missing,

"Oh, no! The card was stolen! I'm so sorry. I'll reverse those charges right away." Marjorie flew back to the counter.

"No, don't do that. Ross reversed the other charges already. He said he'd pay for the flowers for me." Dorie felt heat climbing her neck into her face. "I wondered if the lady who did the ordering came in with the card."

"Well, yes. That's why I didn't question it." Marjorie perched on her bar-height stool. "She chose the flowers to send to you from Ross. Then she used Ross's card. I didn't see anything wrong."

"What did she look like?" Dorie grabbed her

25

legal pad from her bag.

"Blonde-ish, with gray. Long frizzy hair. Not very old, maybe fifties. A little rumpled, like someone who is homeless. Deep blue eyes." Marjorie propped her head on her hand. "I guess I should have known, but Ross had just been in …"

"It's okay, Marjorie. If Riley sent someone down, could you describe her to a sketch artist?"

"Of course. I was so pleased to hear you had set a date for your wedding. I was distracted, I guess." Marjorie pouted.

Dorie came around the counter and hugged her. "It's okay. I'll come back later to pick out wedding flowers."

Marjorie smiled. "I'll give you a discount. Ross grew up here and in Helen. His mom and I were good friends in school."

"I'm sorry I never met her." Dorie stuffed her legal pad back in her bag.

"It was a terrible thing, leaving Ross all alone with his Grandpa MacAvoy. He grew up to be a fine man, though." Marjorie sniffed a little. "I just didn't understand what happened. It's good he's happy. Y'all can start a happier family."

Dorie wasn't sure what to say to that. She knew they died. What's to understand? "I'll see you soon to order those flowers."

As she left the shop, she dialed Ross, since he was supposed to be with Riley anyway.

"Hello, Sweetheart!"

Dorie could hear the smile in his voice. She couldn't help but smile herself. "Hello, my darling man. I just checked with Marjorie about the flower order."

"What did she say? Riley was about to send a guy down to see her."

"Send a sketch artist. It sounds like the woman you gave the money to." Dorie crossed Main Street to the strip mall with the Beacon office. "It is not warmer, is it?"

"I'll tell him. Perhaps I should do the same." Ross spoke to Riley in the background.

"Couldn't hurt. I'm stepping into the office now. Gotta go."

"You know I love you."

His words melted her heart even in the midst of the flurries. "Back at you, sweetheart."

Alexander, one of her fellow reporters in the first set of desks, made smoochy faces at her as she hung up.

"Just stop." She shook her head as she crossed the aisle to her own desk. After divesting her coat and belongings, she had an idea. "Alexander, do you have the police blotter info?"

"Yes, my love. I'll give it to you for a kiss." He held the papers up then yanked them back. "Come on, give us a kiss and a squeeze."

"Not happening, Alex." She reached around him and snagged the papers while he laughed. "You are so immature."

"But I have a good time. Don't forget I helped you out with that mail order rat during the summer." He shook a pencil at her.

"Don't worry. I haven't forgotten. Are you investigating any of these stories?" Dorie sat down in the chair beside him.

"Nah, they're all small potatoes. Mostly shoplifting all over town."

Dorie nodded. "I may have a suspect with a connection." She rushed back to her desk and opened her laptop.

"Dorie, you really shouldn't lead me on so." Alexander looked over the back of his chair. "Throw Ross over and run away with me."

Dorie wadded up a piece of paper, leaned around the flowers, and threw it at him.

Chapter 5

Small towns, where everyone knows everyone else's business …

Dorie did some research, looking at what was stolen at each of the stores in town: food at the grocery; a sleeping bag and a backpack at Hike Daelin, an Appalachian Trail store; boots from the thrift store; a jacket at the big box retail place; and a lantern from an antique shop. Didn't Ross have one of those lanterns in the attic? Maybe they should take it over and sell it to reduce the clutter up there.

Then she dialed Sue Porter. Sue was the town clerk. She took minutes at town hall meetings and kept track of city business.

"Daelin City Hall. Sue speaking."

"Sue, It's Dorie, at the Beacon." She kept forgetting it was a small town. No reason to explain who she was. Especially not to Sue Porter.

"Dorie, how are you? I hear you're getting married Christmas Eve. Congratulations!"

"Yes, how did you hear that? I didn't even know that until this morning." Duh, small town. "Anyway, I wanted some information that I was a little afraid to ask Ross about."

"Ask away, sweetie. If I can help, I will."

"Where is Ross's family buried? Is it easy to find?" Dorie was ready to write down some directions to some obscure church yard on the mountain.

"They're all buried in Daelin in Oaklawn Cemetery not far from Riley's mama."

"I thought they'd be near Helen."

"I think after the autopsies and investigations, Mr. MacAvoy just needed closure and to take care of young Ross."

Autopsies and investigations? What did that mean? "So, Grandpa MacAvoy is buried with his wife?"

"As far as I can reckon. Let me check the files." Sue was only gone for a minute. "Here it is. Grandpa and Grandma MacAvoy are in plot 74 and 75. Ross's daddy is in plot 76. The Ross family plot is nearby, numbers 45-48. Is that all you need?"

"Thank you, Sue. I knew you'd have the answers."

"Toodles, and congrats again."

Dorie hung up and looked at the numbers. Grandparents MacAvoy, Grandparents Ross, Father MacAvoy. Where was Mom MacAvoy? Surely, she wasn't buried in the Ross plot. Dorie looked out at Main Street. Snowing a little harder. She wondered how hard it was to drive up the mountain to Helen in the snow.

Her phone brought her out of her reverie. "Hello?"

"You're invited to my house for takeout before

the roads get too bad." It was Riley.

"Okay, who else is coming? Ross, I assume." Ross wouldn't have it any other way. He'd been so jealous when he'd returned from California.

"Of course. We're about to head for the townhouse. Come on over in about an hour."

"I'll be there." With all this fast food, she'd need a larger size wedding dress, but no way was she confessing such a thing to Marie. It was going to be salads until Christmas.

Dorie took the mystery flowers and her bag out to the car and headed over to the cemetery. She picked up a plot map from the cemetery office and drove the winding roads around the cemetery until she came to Mama McDonough's grave. She pulled flowers from the vase, walked over the snow, and laid four roses from the arrangement on the grave. One each for Riley, Ryker, Ross and herself.

Then she walked the area until she found the Ross family plot. She laid two lilies on each of Ross's grandparents' graves, John and Millicent Ross.

Finally, she approached the MacAvoy plots. An older lady was huddled there, trying to find shelter from the cold wind.

Dorie approached her with caution. "Hi, are you okay?"

The lady startled with her approach. She stood and backed away from the grave where she'd huddled. She was wearing a new AT backpack, boots, and a newish jacket. Could this be the homeless lady Ross had befriended?

"Don't be afraid. I'm not going to hurt you."

Dorie called out to the lady, but she ran away from Dorie. Dorie reached the grave and read the inscription: Andrew Glen MacAvoy Died May 20, 1995. Ross's dad on Ross's fifth birthday. His grandma, Margaret MacAvoy's death was the same day. His grandfather, Andrew MacAvoy's date of death was May 20, 2012, Ross's graduation and birthday. Dorie did not find a grave for Jeanine Ross MacAvoy. She distributed the rest of the flowers among the MacAvoy's graves then walked back to the Ross family plots. The dates of death for both of them was May 20, 1995.

Dorie wondered aloud on her way back to the car. "Lord, what happened on May 20, 1995, that left Ross an orphan and his grandfather all alone to raise him? Where's his mother's grave. What went on in this family?" Ross had never said anything about his family except his grandpa had raised him and there was no one left.

Dorie shivered when she reached the SUV. The snow came down harder. She started the car and headed to Riley's townhouse.

***

Ross stared out Riley's townhouse window watching the snow drift in the complex parking lot. "Where is she? Dorie should have been here by now."

"Relax, buddy. I'm sure she just got caught up on a hot story. She'll be here. If Dorie was in trouble, she'd call you or me." Riley started a pot of coffee to go with their KFC. "She's like a dog with a bone when she's got a story to follow."

"You're right. She probably got caught up in

something." Ross flopped on the couch.

"Actually, I'm thinking I should hire her to work with my detectives. Her investigative abilities could be greatly appreciated." Riley sat down next to Ross. "Also, as a communication person, I could use her for press conferences and police statements."

"You might need a box for her to stand on." Ross covered his mouth. "Did I say that out loud?"

Riley laughed. "Yes, bud, you sure did say that out loud. Good thing Dorie's not here to hear you."

"It was interesting meeting her family. Her brothers are tall, over six feet, and thin. Her mom and dad are tallish as well." Ross got out his phone and scrolled through his photos. "See, Dorie is maybe five foot two. Here's a picture with her and her family."

Riley took his phone. "She also has different coloring. It's almost like she doesn't exactly belong."

"It's odd, but her family is great." Ross took back his phone as he received a text from Dorie. He read it to Riley. "On my way. Be there in a couple minutes. Love, Dorie."

"See I told you it was okay. Coffee?" Riley headed for the kitchen.

Ross followed. "I'll go ahead and fix mine and Dorie's."

The knock at the door caused both Ross and Riley to yell, "Come in!"

"Whose house is this anyway?" Riley threw his hands in the air. "I know you're living here right now, but don't get used to it. You gotta go home eventually."

Ross headed for the door. "Sorry."

Dorie opened the door and entered, shaking the snow from her coat and stomping her feet. "This looks like we brought snow with us from St. Louis. I thought it didn't snow in the South."

"The mountains are different." Ross took her coat and draped it over a chair. He enfolded her in a bear hug. "You're cold. What have you been doing?"

"Poking my nose in your family business." Dorie hugged him back on tiptoes. I went by Oaklawn to put my flowers on your family's graves. I also put four roses on Mama Mary's, Riley."

"Thanks." Riley called out from the kitchen.

Ross held her like he would never let go. Some time, he had to tell her about his big family secret, the one everyone in town knew except Dorie. And she'd figure it out soon enough.

"I saw your homeless lady there, Ross. She was on your dad's grave."

Horror gripped his heart. It couldn't be her, could it?

Riley shot him a poignant look.

Ross shook his head. No, it wasn't time to tell her the nightmarish tale of his fifth birthday party.

Chapter 6

Spending the night …

Dorie caught the look Ross and Riley exchanged. While she clearly had no idea what it meant, it also was clear they didn't plan to share. She'd ask when she was alone with Ross. Something very bad happened in 1995. She knew she could find out more without Ross telling her. Small towns. She could find out what happened eventually when she found the right source. Marjorie had hinted at something today.

"Coffee, love?" Ross was looking down at her. "You spaced out for a minute. Everything okay."

"Yes, on coffee. Probably, on being okay." Dorie squirmed out of Ross's embrace and headed to the kitchen to help Riley.

Dorie hugged Riley and whispered into his ear. "What isn't he telling me about his fifth birthday?"

"I was there. It was something I'll never forget, but it's his story to tell, Dorie." Riley handed her a coffee cup. "Don't push is my advice."

"Whispering in the kitchen will make the fiancé jealous, you know. Come eat while it's semi-hot." Ross flipped on the news.

Dorie and Riley joined him on the couch and chatted about each story. When the news was over, Dorie decided she should leave before the snow got any worse.

"Guys, I need to head out."

"Are you sure you're comfortable driving up the mountain in the snow?" Ross jumped to help her with her coat.

"I learned how to drive in St. Louis and spent four years in Blacksburg, Virginia. A little snow doesn't scare me." She flipped her scarf, and it grazed Ross's face. "Sorry, love."

Ross grabbed her and snuggled into her scarf for a kiss. "Don't take chances."

"Of course not." She struggled out of his embrace and opened the door.

Six inches had accumulated on top the SUV. The parking lot had drifts a foot deep.

Dorie turned around and looked at Ross and Riley. "New plan. Can I pull up a floor to sleep on tonight? I'll check with Melody about letting Star out." She dialed Melody as she headed to the kitchen.

The guys ran to look out the door.

"You're staying here, or I'm going with you." Ross called out to her. "No way you're taking that mountain road tonight alone."

Riley leaned on the corner of the entrance to the kitchen. "I'm actually going to agree with Ross on this one. You know, I always side with you being as independent as possible, but I don't want to fish your fancy new SUV off the side of the mountain."

"Thanks for the confidence boost."

Ross stuck his head in around Riley. "What did

Melody say?"

"She just let Star out and said, 'Tain't fit night for man nor beast. Stay in Daelin.' So, I guess I'm outnumbered."

The guys both nodded at her.

"Well, show me to my floor space. I'm pretty tired, another reason not to drive up the mountain." Dorie took off her coat and scarf. Ross hung it in the coat closet for her.

"Take my bed, Dorie. I won't feel comfortable with you on the floor. I'll even put fresh sheets on it." Riley headed upstairs to the bedrooms not even waiting to hear her protests.

"Sleep well, my love." Ross gave her a sweet good night kiss. "I'll be down here on the couch."

Dorie gave him another kiss, then she climbed the stairs after Riley.

He was already stripping the bed when she entered his bedroom.

"I feel bad taking your bed. Plus, it just feels wrong." Dorie leaned against the doorframe as she watched him work.

"No worries, darling Dorie. I will not encroach on you in any way. My best friend is downstairs, and you are essentially his wife." He spread fresh sheets on the mattress. "Your relationship to him is sacrosanct. No way would I attempt to interfere."

"Good to know. Where will you sleep?" Dorie watched him spread a blanket and a quilt on the bed.

"In case you get cold. I'll be next door in the second bedroom, using my sleeping bag." Riley reached up into the closet and pulled down a well-worn green sleeping bag. "Don't worry. I'll be warm in this baby."

"Good night, Riley." She gave him a hug, which he returned.

***

Ross listened at the bottom of the stairs. He knew he could trust Dorie, but once he'd left for California, Riley had become quite involved in caring for her. He thought Riley'd fallen in love with Dorie. Part of Ross still stung at the idea of his best friend trying to take Dorie away from him while he was out of Georgia.

Ross heard Riley leave the bedroom. He appeared at the top of the steps.

"Everything's fine. She's closed in the bedroom alone. You needn't worry." Riley sat down on the top step. "She's yours. You win."

"You still want her." Ross felt bad stating the obvious, like rubbing salt in fresh wounds. "I know how that feels. It's hard not to feel threatened."

"Bring your sleeping bag up here and sleep on the floor beside me." Riley's tone was edgy. "You can trust me."

Ever since Riley's mom's funeral, Ross had felt in competition with Riley for Dorie's affections. Dorie had nearly been run over in the graveyard by Riley's brother because he thought it would hurt Riley. Ross had barely saved her from the impact. The fist fight Riley and Ross had after that had given their friendship a couple of black eyes too.

"I'm okay down here, just in case someone tries to come in the front or back door." Ross swallowed his pride. "I trust you, bro."

"So, you should." Riley stood and stalked back

to the bedroom across the hall from Ross's fiancée.

Ross got out his bedroll and spread it on the couch. He looked out on the fresh-fallen snow, which illuminated the otherwise dark night by reflecting the streetlights. Beautiful. He turned out the lights, excepting the light over the stove. Then he slipped between the sheets fully clothed in case Dorie needed him in the night.

It was three when he heard the footfall on the steps. Must be Dorie, five foot two and a hundred pounds, maybe. Riley sounds louder. He listened as she crept down the stairs until visible by the kitchen light.

"What's up, Dorie?" Ross called quietly, so he wouldn't startle her. She seemed on edge a lot of the time these days.

"I didn't mean to wake you." Dorie came over to the couch and sat on the edge. "I had a nightmare about your fifth birthday party."

"I have nightmares about my fifth birthday even now." Could he tell her the whole truth about that day? "Can I help?" He opened the sheets, and she slid in next to him.

"Is this a bad idea?" She was very quiet and very small, like a church mouse compared to him.

"We're both fully clothed, love. I think we can handle it. What do you want to know?" Ross held her to him. "This is not a topic to make love to, trust me."

Chapter 7

Ghostly tales from long ago …

I lost my whole family that day except Grandpa." Ross shivered, though having Dorie close certainly warmed up the couch. The tale was painful to remember, much less to tell. "It changed my whole life. It probably changed me forever."

"Riley said he was there, but he wouldn't tell me. He said it was your story to tell." She snuggled in closer. "He also told me not to ask."

"Glad to see you take advice so well, girl." He tickled her to lighten the mood. "Mom said at age five I could have five friends for my party. We bought plates, cups, and napkins with a firetruck on them all. Riley was there along with four other friends from kindergarten."

"A firetruck?"

"Dad was a fireman. He was away a lot, but he got off in time for my party. He took a bunch of pictures before …" He stopped. He wasn't sure he could tell her of the horror that occurred. "He took one of Mom and said she was beautiful."

"So, you wanted to be a fireman like your dad?"

Ross appreciated the diversion from the story. "Always before that day."

"So that's why you went to help plant trees after the fires in California." Dorie kissed his cheek.

"Partly. After my nursery business burned to the ground, I needed to be helpful somewhere, too." Chalk that one up to the infamous Hilde, too.

Before he realized it, he was shaking, and tears were running down his face into his beard. He sat up, holding Dorie to him. "I can't do it tonight. It's not because I don't want you to know. It's just …"

Dorie wrapped her arms around him. "It's okay, Ross. It's okay. I understand PTSD, remember? You're here with me, and Riley's upstairs."

On cue Riley poked his head down the stairs. "Everything okay in here? Don't make me be the morality police."

"Come on down." Ross stilled the shaking and wiped his face. He kissed Dorie. "I'm sorry, darling."

"Coffee?" Dorie jumped up and headed to the kitchen. "Brrr. The floor's cold."

"What do you expect? There's like a foot of snow out there." Riley peered out the kitchen window while Dorie set up the coffeepot. He whispered in her ear. "Did you have to ask him?"

Even though Riley whispered, Ross heard every word. "No need to whisper. I can hear you anyway."

Ross entered the kitchen while stretching and tousling his hair. "It's really early, guys."

Dorie stood in the corner, watching the coffee brew. Ross pushed Riley out of the way and reached for her. He stood behind her and wrapped his arms around her until the coffee finished.

***

Dorie bundled up and headed to the SUV to

remove the maybe six inches of snow from it. The sun was bright and warm. Most of the snow on the car had already melted. Ross followed her out and brushed off the other side. People in the complex had already left slushy tracks in the snowy parking lot.

Ross came to her and kissed her. "You go on to work. I'll head up to the house in the truck to check on Star and make sure everything's okay."

Dorie nodded and kissed him back. "I'll go up later today and work from there. Should I bring up lunch?"

"Nah, I'll swing through the grocery and pick up ingredients for chili and grilled cheese."

Dorie looked deep into his blue eyes. "Are you okay? I mean, about this morning."

Ross nodded. "It will never be all right. I've learned how to live without letting it dominate my life. Just like you and your late fiancé Elliott, forward is better than looking backward."

Dorie kissed him again. "I love you. Don't forget."

"How could I forget? When we marry, you'll be my family. I won't be alone again." Ross hugged her and went to brush the snow off his grandpa's old, rusty truck.

It dawned on Dorie that his truck and house were all he had left of his family. She remembered the row of graves, all but one buried due to a singular event at Ross's fifth birthday party. How could anyone ever get past such a tragedy? When he was done and in the truck, she started the SUV and waited to be sure the truck actually started. When it did, Ross waved to her, and she drove over the crunchy tire tracks until she reached Main Street. Instead of heading into the Daily Beacon office, she headed to Java Joint.

As Dorie entered, Angela called out, "Mocha double shot. Anything else?"

"Sure, a muffin sounds good. And a minute of your time."

Dorie took her regular seat in the back-corner booth. She sighed. What if Angela didn't say yes? Who else could she ask?

Angela arrived with the coffee and a muffin. "What's going on, darling?"

"I need a matron of honor. Could you be her?" Dorie held her breath, hoping she'd say yes. "Please say yes, Angela."

Angela shrieked. "Yes! Christmas Eve? Absolutely!"

"I'm heading to Atlanta on Saturday with Marie to Lori's Bridal. Can you come with us?"

Angela grabbed Dorie's hand. "'Say Yes to the Dress-Atlanta'? Yes, I can't wait to see that place. I watch that show all the time. Just say what time, and I'm ready to go."

Someone dinged the bell at the counter. "On my way! Thank you, Dorie. Thank you for asking me."

Dorie smiled. Is it wrong that my best girlfriend in Georgia is my barista? Probably. I need to make more friends.

Chapter 8

Finding out more about Ross …

A s soon as Dorie arrived at the Beacon, she closed herself in the microfiche room and pulled the tape from 1995. She threaded the tape and zoomed it through the machine until it reached May 20, 1995. The headline she was looking for appeared on the screen, "Family Slaughtered During Boy's Birthday Party." The picture showed a scattered and destroyed birthday party with five-year-old Ross in the midst. Riley was at his side, and they were hugging. Blood stained Ross's shirt and face. The picture alone put Dorie's heart in her throat. Knowing the little boys in the picture brought tears to her eyes. Who could do such a thing?

Dorie enlarged the article and printed the screen. She replaced the tape and turned off the hot, ancient machine. Then she picked up the printed pages and headed back to her desk. On her desk was a copy of the day's Beacon. The police sketch of the homeless lady appeared on the front-page accompanying Dorie's article about the thefts. The lady's face seemed familiar, something around the eyes. Of course, Dorie had seen her yesterday. Of course, she'd seem familiar.

Dorie set the paper aside and read the printed microfiche article about Ross's party gone wrong.

Birthday Party Tragedy

Little Ross MacAvoy had his 5-year birthday party on Saturday. He had firetrucks for his theme. His daddy Daelin Firefighter Glen MacAvoy took pictures while Ross blew out the candles on his fire truck cake. Before the party was over, however, all the MacAvoy and Ross family members were dead, killed with the ice pick used to create ice for the Kool-Aid. The alleged attacker was Ross's mother, Jeanine Ross MacAvoy, who also sustained wounds in the frenzy. Mrs. MacAvoy is in Emory Hospital, Atlanta. The boy's grandfather, Andrew MacAvoy, received minor wounds and survives his wife, Maggie, and his son Glen. He has been named guardian for the five-year-old boy. Also deceased are John and Millicent Ross, Jeanine MacAvoy's parents. None of the children at the party was attacked.

Tears ran down Dorie's face. No wonder he didn't want to talk about this day. No five-year-old should suffer so much grief. This article didn't say whether his mom survived. Ugh, more time at the microfiche machine unless Google could help. Dorie opened the laptop, but she couldn't make herself look at any more of this horror. Time for a break.

Dorie grabbed her coat from the back of her chair, and her phone and wallet from her bag. The bell jingled on the door as she went out into the sunshine and melting snow. She walked up Main Street to Madame's, the formal dress shop in Daelin. It was the only place in town to rent tuxedos. She knew they carried a few gowns in store, but she was headed to Atlanta in just a few days. No need to get caught up in trying on dresses during the workday.

Dorie wandered into the shop and glanced at the dress on the mannequin. Being short was not going to help her land a dress in the next three weeks.

"Can I help you? Dorie Hudson, am I right? I just love your writing. It's very real and no nonsense."

The lady was tall and willowy, not someone who could necessarily understand the real figure problems of a short, somewhat curvy girl.

"I'm getting married Christmas Eve, yes, this year in three plus weeks."

"Oh, yes. Ross was in here yesterday but couldn't comprehend the array of options available in a tuxedo." The lady started sorting through dresses and pulling several out. "Now you will want a somewhat simple style. Too much bling would just weigh you down, if you know what I mean."

Dorie wasn't at all sure what that could mean. "Explain."

"Bling would accentuate your curves, usually a good thing for a bride." She winked at her. "But you are so short, it would make you look short and stout."

Dorie shook her head. "Not the look anyone would want."

"We'll have to shorten any of these gowns, which would mean cutting off any hew details, that means no trains or lace or edging because there's no time for extreme alterations." The lady pulled a dress. "Here's one you might could use."

It was not like anything Dorie hoped to wear on her wedding day. "I don't think that's what I would want. Anyway, I came in to look at tuxedos."

The lady seemed to melt at this remark. "Oh. I see. You can look at the books, and I can look through my collection again."

"That sounds fine. I'm looking for a Christmas look for the guys. Maybe a red plaid?"

Dorie walked to the back of the store to the table holding bridal and tuxedo books. She found the holiday looks and chose a red plaid vest and bow tie with a white shirt. She chose a regular black tuxedo. After filling out the paperwork, she texted a picture to Ross and Riley. It was a start.

After gathering her things at the Beacon, she took the mountain road to Helen, GA.

Chapter 9

Visiting the attic …

Ross was stirring a big pot of chili when Dorie's text arrived. "Oh, no, no, no." Before he had a chance to text Riley, his phone rang.

"Seriously, red and white generic plaid?" Riley sounded insulted. "It feels like a cookie cutter Hallmark Christmas movie. We be descended from the Scots, me lad. Tartan plaid. That's what we should be wearing."

"Relax. I have a better idea. While Dorie's gone Saturday, let's make some formal dress decisions of our own." Ross took a spoon and tasted the chili. "I'll probably have plenty of this chili left. Come over later. Dorie doesn't eat much."

"Bring it down the mountain tonight."

"We'll see. I may need to stay here tonight. Dorie was pretty freaked out this morning."

Riley laughed. "You can tell yourself that. You just don't want to sleep on my couch."

"Maybe not. Can you blame me?" Ross checked his watch. "Let me go. I want to check on something in the attic before Dorie gets home."

Ross turned off the burner and covered the pot.

Then he headed out to the garage and up into the attic. He searched through the crowd of memories until he found his Grandmother Ross's cedar chest. He opened it and the pungent smell of cedar escaped. That's where he found what he was looking for: Grandfather Ross's wedding kilt with all the accoutrements, including a full tartan.

This Ross hunting plaid was shades of green with red highlights. Ross knew their clan had several versions of the plaid. If he was going to wear a Christmas plaid, by golly it would be authentic. He tried on the Prince Charlie jacket. It actually fit. All he needed was a white shirt as long as the moths hadn't attacked the wool. He heard Dorie's car door slam. He stuffed the outfit back in the cedar chest. He hurried down the stairs and got to the front door as she opened it.

"Oh my!" Dorie grabbed onto his arms. "I didn't expect a grand reception."

"Welcome home, milady." Ross took her in his arms and dipped her into a kiss. "So glad you are home."

"Wow! What a welcome. The chili smells great!" Dorie took off her coat and hung it up. "What do you think about the wedding tuxes?"

"They're okay, but I think I might have a better idea after all. Okay with you?"

"What? You don't like it." Dorie's face fell. "I guess I should have taken more time on it. I can go back and change it."

"No. I have a great idea. Riley and I have this in the bag."

Dorie gave him a puzzled look. "Should I be

afraid to see what you're wearing when I get to the bottom of the stairs?"

"Trust me." Ross grabbed her and pulled her to him. "I love you. I would not mess this up." He kissed her and led her into the kitchen.

After lunch, Dorie took her laptop to where she could see the mountains.

Ross checked email and watched her while she worked. He couldn't comprehend how he could have fallen so quickly and completely in love with someone in less than six months. If he was being honest with himself, he knew that the morning she'd thrown coffee on him had been the moment he'd felt that she was the one. Before then, he hadn't believed in love at first sight or the idea of soulmates. He had also planned to never let anyone in, never marry, never have a family. After what had happened with his mom and dad, how could he ever let anyone in?

Lord, You are mighty and redeeming. Thank You for these normal loving moments with Dorie. Thank You for bringing her into my life. Thank You for putting her literally under my nose. Help us make a life that is pleasing to You. Help me be the man I need to be for her. Help her know, without a shadow of a doubt, how much I love her.

"Ross, are you okay?"

He snapped out of his reverie. "I'm great, right here with you."

Her look seemed puzzled but somehow satisfied. "I love you too."

"What if we wrote our own vows?" Ross could barely believe he even wanted to do that. "Are you interested?"

Dorie came to him and sat beside him. "Is that something you want to do?"

"I think I do. At least I want to make some remarks before the 'I do's." Ross wondered if he'd be able to speak at all after she descended those stairs in whatever she ended up choosing. "I want to tell you before witnesses how much I love you."

"I think everyone knows." She leaned over and gave him a kiss.

"That reminds me, we should go into the attic and find that veil I remember being there." Ross jumped up from the sofa, dragging her behind him.

"You are really excited about the wedding, aren't you?" Dorie seemed amused.

Ross smiled. "Of course, I am. I get to claim my forever love. We become one."

"And we finally can become husband and wife physically too?" Dorie followed him up the attic stairs.

"That, too. But it's definitely more than that. I love you, need you, want you. You're the woman God made just for me. It's time to make it permanent." Ross avoided the cedar chest with the kilt ensemble. "I think it's over here."

Dorie joined Ross at the cedar chest he indicated. He opened it, releasing that cedar aroma. This one was his Grandma MacAvoy's chest. Pearls, a quilt, a baby blanket, a doll, finally a box marked wedding veil. He handed it to her.

Dorie opened the box and folded back the tissue paper, once white now champagne colored. The white veil glistened with pearls studded throughout.

Silver beads were scattered over the lace that covered the entire edge of the veil. The comb was just behind the lace edge so that when Dorie stuck it into her hair, the lace edge framed her face, cascaded over her shoulders, and fell to the floor all along the sheer tulle.

Ross caught his breath. She was beautiful. And she would wear that veil at their wedding. No way could she not like it. "There's a mirror over here." Ross pulled the full-length mirror from the corner, so Dorie could see what he saw.

"Oh, Ross. It's beautiful." Her voice caught in her throat. "As long as we can get the smell of cedar out of it, I'd be delighted to wear your grandma's veil. Let's look at the pearls, too." She opened the box and gasped. The necklace was a triple strand with a jewel-encrusted clasp.

Ross picked them out of the box and put them on her. He smiled at her in the mirror. Beautiful, even in jeans. "Definitely."

She nodded and returned his smile.

"We can bring it downstairs and let it air out. The bridal shop should know how to freshen the veil. Go ahead and bring the pearls down and put them in your dresser. They're yours now."

Dorie hugged him. "It's too much to take in, Ross. All I really want is you. Everything else is so much more than I deserve."

Ross hugged her back. "On that, we must disagree. You deserve all God brings into our lives. I hope to give you everything you want that I can."

They replaced the veil and pearls in the boxes and carried them to the second-floor landing. The door there opened at the end of the hall.

***

Dorie could not believe the blessings God had rained down on her. Most of them began with Ross – love, protection, a home, a new vehicle, a wedding, the items from the attic, his friend Riley. It was so much more than she'd ever expected to have when she moved to Daelin. In their bedroom-to-be, she slid the pearls into a drawer in the dresser for safekeeping.

Dorie hung the veil on a hanger to allow it to air out. She'd check with Lori's Bridals, the Say Yes to the Dress, Atlanta, bridal shop. In fact, Dorie would take the veil and the pearls with her on Saturday. All she needed was a dress and shoes. And the patience to wait for Christmas Eve.

Chapter 10

The unexpected cut …

Don't you need to get going for your trip to Atlanta?" Ross called up the steps to Dorie. "Riley just pulled up."

"I know. I've got to get the veil and pearls."

Ross could hear her steps scurrying around the upstairs. He opened the door for Riley before he even rang the bell. Star came running to greet him.

"Oh, no!" The high-pitched wail sent Ross up the stairs, two at a time. "Who would have done this?"

Ross arrived in time to see Dorie lifting the veil from its perch. "What's wrong?"

She turned around and held it up. "Someone has slashed it from top to bottom. It's ruined. Who would do such a thing?" Tears streamed down her face. "Whoever it was had a knife. Either or both of us could have been killed."

"No one's been in this house besides you, me, Riley, and Star. None of us would destroy that vintage veil." He stepped toward her and crushed a pearl on the floor that had escaped from the damaged veil. "Take it with you. Perhaps it can be repaired. Or just buy a new one. Time is short."

Riley came into the room. "Who would do such a thing? How did they get into the house?'

"Did you change the locks like I suggested?" Dorie reached out to Ross. "You didn't, did you? If you did, you'd have given me a new key."

"No, I didn't. No one else has a key." Ross felt the blood rising into his face. "I will do it today after Riley and I take care of our wedding errand."

Dorie looked disappointed in him. He was also disappointed, in the loss of the veil but also the fact that someone was accessing the house without their permission. Was he or she sabotaging the wedding? What was going on?

Dorie's phone rang. "It's Marie. I have to go."

Ross snagged her before she could leave the room. "Try not to worry about this. Have a wonderful day finding the perfect dress. Don't worry about the price." He kissed her then let her go. "I love you."

"I'll try." Her mouth said yes, but her eyes were damp and said no. "I love you too."

As soon as she left, Riley and Ross got in Riley's cruiser and headed for a different shop in Atlanta, Atlanta Kilts.

"What is happening in your house, Ross?" Riley pulled out onto the road down the mountain, heading for the highway. "I don't understand how someone can get into your house with both of you there."

"I know. I don't understand it either, but it's not a figment of Dorie's imagination. I doubt Dorie would take a knife to the veil, even if she were sleepwalking."

"Yeah. I guess that's one explanation. How about ghosts? Your family may not be resting after what happened at your party."

Ross gave Riley a hard look. "We're Christians here. Ghosts are not part of our belief system."

"I know. I know. But what if?"

"No, I can't accept it was a ghost. I'd be more afraid that it's someone who didn't die that day." Ross shivered. "I don't even want to think about that."

"Perhaps we should be thinking about that. Ignoring the possibility of it being your mom won't be a satisfactory response. What if it is her? Dorie could be in danger."

Ross shook his head. "Surely she's dead or still locked away."

"Maybe I should look into it for you."

***

Ross and Riley pulled up in front of Atlanta Kilts at opening time. Ross pulled his grandfather's kilt ensemble from the back seat, and they entered after the door was unlocked.

"G'morning, lads." The customer service man was dressed in full kilt regalia. Bagpipe music played throughout the store, lending an atmosphere of Scotland. "Aye, I see ye have yer own kilt. I be Liam, at your service today."

"From a cedar chest in the attic. My grandfather's kilt." Ross felt an emotional response to the historical significance of the Ross kilt in his hand. "It may not be in good enough shape for my wedding. My best man needs a kilt as well."

"A Ross hunting kilt tartan. Ye be a Ross, then."

"Actually, I'm Ross MacAvoy. My mother's family was Ross. My father was a MacAvoy."

"Aye, we don't have a MacAvoy tartan. When is the wedding, Ross?"

"Three weeks, Christmas Eve." Ross held his breath. The last thing he wanted was to hear the wedding was too soon. "Can you help us?"

"Aye. Let me check on the Ross ensembles. The green should be well-received for Christmas Eve." Liam took Ross's grandfather's kilt from him. "I'll look over the legacy wear and see if ye truly want to wear it on yer special day."

Liam went behind a curtain. Ross looked around him. He'd never seen so much plaid in one place. Riley was leafing through a catalog of tartans. The more Ross saw, the surer he was that a kilt was the perfect thing for the wedding. Hopefully, Dorie would be surprised in a good way. Should he worry about the shape of his calves?

"What do you think, Riley? Am I crazy to think Dorie will be okay with us in kilts instead of tuxedoes?"

"Dorie was pretty adamant about you wearing a tux, bro." Riley showed the McDonough tartan to Ross. "Should I buy one for special occasions? You and me, kilts about town."

"Don't think we have much opportunity for such, Riley." Ross walked back to the counter, edgy about the condition of his grandfather's kilt ensemble, edgy about doing something different than what Dorie wanted on Christmas Eve. The last thing he wanted was to ruin the day.

Liam finally appeared from behind the curtain

with the kilt ensemble and a fresh white shirt. "I believe we can clean and mend this. Let's see how it fits." He led Ross to a dressing room and helped him put on the various pieces appropriately. He supplied the missing bits as well: socks, shoes, kilt pins, brooch.

Ross emerged from the dressing room in full formal kilt ensemble. Liam began checking the fit and measuring with his tape.

"The shoulders are a wee tight, but I think they'll do for an evening. Letting them out would probably show the newly exposed fabric next to the older fabric. The kilt is a bit loose in the waist, but we can fix that." He rearranged the tartan thrown over Ross's shoulder held by the brooch. "Remember that once we clean it, it should be brighter seeming. Take a look, Ross. What do ye think?"

Liam led Ross to a trifold mirror. Ross couldn't believe his eyes. It felt natural to wear the kilt of his ancestors. The shades of green shot through with red looked perfect for a Christmas wedding. With his sandy hair and red beard, he looked like someone from Braveheart. Surely Dorie could appreciate this look on him at their wedding.

Riley appeared in the mirror behind him. "Aye, that's a manly look, Ross. Who knew a skirt could be so fetching on a man?"

"You're next, bro."

Liam produced a measuring tape. After taking Riley's measurements, Liam headed back behind the curtain.

"Want me to take some quick photos, my liege?" Riley took out his cell phone and snapped a few from several angles. "It's a good look on you, Ross."

Liam appeared with a sample outfit for Riley to try on. "McDonough is Irish from County Cork. You can choose to wear the McDonough, which we must source elsewhere, or wear the same kilt as the groom."

Ross walked around the store, feeling more and more comfortable in the outfit. Dorie would love it. He needed to ask about two more things, a Ross tartan sash and brooch for Dorie to wear with her dress after the ceremony and a handfasting ribbon with which to "tie the knot".

"Well, what do you think, laddie?" Riley emerged from the dressing room outfitted in the Ross kilt.

"It's great, bro. I love it. What are your thoughts about it?" Ross grinned as Riley checked himself out in the trifold mirror.

"I love it. I'm sorely tempted to buy a McDonough outfit to store away for special occasions."

Liam joined Ross. "What do ye think, Ross? Is it a go?"

"Aye. I need a few more things. A Ross sash for my bride to wear afterwards with a brooch and a ribbon for the handfasting." Ross followed Liam over to the jewelry case. He chose a double-heart brooch with a garnet in silver for Dorie. Then Liam described how they would make a handfasting ribbon from a strip of the Ross tartan with a ribbon and charm.

Liam totaled all the merchandise: white shirt, socks, shoes, sash and brooch for Dorie, the handfasting ribbon, and the cleaning and repair on Grandfather's kilt ensemble.

Liam made some phone calls and found a place to get the County Cork kilt for the McDonough. Then he totaled the purchase for Riley who also went ahead and purchased his kilt, fly plaid, shirt, socks, and shoes. They arranged to return the weekend before Christmas for the rest of the items.

By noon, Ross and Riley were on the highway headed for Helen, Georgia.

DIANE E. TATUM

Chapter 11

Selecting a dress …

Dorie, Marie, and Angela arrived at Bridals by Lori before opening and were whisked into an appointment area. Lori herself brought sample dresses to the dressing room she had chosen based on Marie's suggestions.

"Dorie, welcome to Bridals by Lori." An associate named Joanie greeted her and began sorting through the dresses. "Lace? Ballgown? Mermaid? Pearls and beads? How do you see yourself in your dream wedding?"

Dorie opened the bag with the veil. "This was my fiance's grandma's veil. I loved it. Someone tried to destroy it. Is there any hope for it?"

"I can take it downstairs to our seamstresses to see what they say. To do this would take a long time, I'm afraid." Joanie carefully fingered the veil. "We might have something similar. Remember if the dress has a lace edge like this veil, it will take longer to alter the dress shorter for you."

All the dresses Dorie loved had that lace around the bottom. However, the dresses were all too long for someone so short. She tried on one and went out to show Marie and Angela.

"Oh, Dorie, it's beautiful." Angela jumped up and had to hug her. "This has got to be the one, isn't it?"

The dress was gorgeous lace including a wide lace embellishment at the hem. The yoke was sheer with lace embellishments. Dorie stood on the pedestal, and the dress hung down in front a good six inches.

"I love this dress, but it's too long." Dorie felt tears forming. First the veil, now the dresses were too long. Did that mean the wedding should be postponed?

Joanie stepped up to address Marie and Angela. "I explained that it's hard to hem a dress like this quickly. The seamstress would have to remove the lace, shorten the gown, then reapply the lace."

"Oh, Dorie." Angela sulked on the couch. "It's perfect otherwise."

"Try on another dress." Marie was undeterred.

Dorie tried on four more dresses that could not be altered in time for Christmas Eve or simply didn't work: a mermaid that the body was too long, a ballgown with a poof-y skirt that was too big for someone so small, a narrow shift dress with no shape that didn't fit Dorie's curves nor height, a halter dress that the halter was too long to hold her in. How could she have any dress shortened in time?

Taking off the last dress, Dorie sat in a corner of the dressing room and cried. Owner Lori hurried into the room and sat next to Dorie. "Joanie says you are having a hard time."

"The dress I love can't be hemmed in time. The

rest don't look good on me." Lori handed the box of Kleenex to her. "I don't think my wedding will happen Christmas Eve after all."

"Show me the dress you love. Try it on for me, Dorie."

Lori helped her into the lace dress with the large lace-edged hem and train. "It is definitely your dress. What's in this box?"

Dorie opened the pearls.

"How would you feel about an ivory dress? The pearls would look lovely on an ivory dress."

Dorie shrugged. "Why not?"

"Wait here. Don't give up hope." She turned to her assistant. "Joanie, go down to alterations. There's a dress that wasn't picked up that might just fit Miss Dorie."

Joanie left them.

"It will be okay. We are determined to give our brides what they need and want for their big day. Look what I brought you." She unzipped a long bag and pulled out a veil that looked very much like Grandma MacAvoy's.

Dorie stood, and Lori put the comb in her hair and arranged the veil.

"Look in the mirror. What do you think?"

Dorie couldn't believe how close the veil was to the original. "This is white though. It won't be right with an ivory dress."

"No worries, Miss Dorie. It comes in ivory too."

Joanie appeared in the dressing room with a bag. She unzipped the garment bag and pulled out the exact dress that Dorie loved, except in ivory. Lori helped her into it while Joanie went for the ivory veil to match it.

Dorie turned around and gasped. It was beautiful and just the right length.

"Shall we go show the ladies?" Lori held the curtain back, so Dorie could go to the showroom.

Angela cried out. "It's perfect! You must get this dress!"

Dorie grinned as she stepped onto the pedestal in front of the mirrors. Joanie brought the ivory veil and placed it in her hair. The ivory lace edged the veil to the floor and around the entire edge of the veil. It had sparkly beads in the lace, like Grandma MacAvoy's. The only thing missing were the pearl accents.

Dorie couldn't believe her eyes. She looked like a bride. Growing up with three big brothers, she'd been a tomboy most of her life. Getting a job as an investigative reporter fit her since she wasn't afraid to get dirty. But this, this surprised even her.

Lori brought out the pearl strands and placed it on her.

Angela was right, as usual. It was perfect.

"Well, what do you say to this dress?" Lori prompted her for her signature response.

"Yes. I'm saying yes to this dress."

Everyone cheered. Mayhem reigned in the rest of the store with brides snatching dresses off the racks at cut rate prices. Dorie felt peace. And it was worth whatever the price this dress cost. Ross had said not to worry about the price, after all.

Dorie and Angela then headed to the bridesmaids' shop. Marie joined the mayhem on the other side of the store to write about it for the Beacon.

"Pick out a red dress, one you love and could be used over and over again." Dorie hugged her friend. "Don't worry about the cost. Let me buy it for you."

Angela let out a pleased eek! and headed for the red dress area. While she looked, Lori talked about the cost of the ivory gown.

"Now, Dorie, the gown you love has been paid for except for the alterations. So, I'm going to charge you for the alterations and the veil." Lori wrote up the sale ticket. "But I have a thought about the veil. Would you like one of our seamstresses to sew the pearls from the old veil onto your new one?"

"That could be done in time for Christmas Eve?" Dorie was stunned. It was more than she thought she could even ask.

"It could." She named a price for labor. "And it could be done by the weekend before the wedding."

"Yes. I would love that." Dorie's eyes filled with tears of joy.

Meanwhile Joanie was helping Angela choose from the red dresses that were available to take home that day. Finally, Angela came out to show Dorie what she had picked.

"Angie, it's beautiful." Dorie jumped up to hug her. "Is this the dress you love? Remember, you're not paying for this dress. I insist."

"I love it. Thank you, Dorie. I feel like a princess in this dress."

The dress was shirred lux chiffon at the bodice with a sheer yoke, similar to Dorie's gown, and a slightly shirred skirt from the waist to the floor. It had a front slit. The color was called Cabernet. It was demure, a dress she could wear to a dressy dinner or party. Even better, it was in the sample sale and fit Angela to a tee.

While Angela changed back to her jeans, Dorie settled the bill with Lori.

It was a good thing Dorie had brought the blue SUV. Putting two gowns in the back without scrunching either used all the room available with half the back seat down. Marie got her story, so the morning was a huge success.

They had lunch at a tearoom Marie knew before heading back to Daelin and Helen.

Marie stood with a frosty mug of fruit tea. "To the bride, Dorie may your wedding be everything you envision."

"Here, here." Angela raised her glass and the ladies drank to the toast.

Chapter 12

Coming home to a mess …

Ross knew before he got out of Riley's SUV that something bad had happened. The front door was standing open. Luckily, Star was in her crate or she would be lost. He ran to the door.

"Stop, Ross!" Riley jumped out of the vehicle and ran to hold him back from entering the house. "Don't go in. Let me get the pros in first."

Ross stopped. He could hear Star whining and yipping. "It's okay, girl. I'm here."

Riley called in the break-in to Helen PD.

Ross shoved his hands in his pockets and headed around the house. He had assured Dorie that she was safe. He hadn't really believed that Dorie heard someone in the house. He had failed to keep her safe. Somebody had slashed the veil in the bedroom next to where she slept! What was happening? He was in the backyard when he heard the sirens. He picked up Star's ball and slung it into the corner of the fence then headed to the front to greet the police, again.

When he reached the front, Riley was already in deep conversation with Ross's friend, Bobby.

"There he is. Ross, what's happenin' here?"

Ross shook Bobby's hand. "I wish I knew. New locks shortly, before nightfall. In fact, I think I'll send Dorie to Andrews' guest cottage. If she has a wedding dress, I can't take a chance on someone ruining it."

"Probably a good idea. She will be nervous after the veil incident." Riley leaned against his car. "Bobby, why don't you and me check out the house?" Riley stood up and got his service revolver from the gun safe in his car. "Ross, stay here until we give the all-clear."

The two police officers entered the house with weapons drawn. He could hear their loud 'Clear!" calls as each checked different parts of the house. He didn't want to call Dorie before he saw the house for himself.

Finally, Riley called out to him. "Come on in and tell us what's wrong."

When Ross got to the door, Bobby handed him a pair of gloves and shoe covers. Ross could tell standing at the front door that someone had trashed the house. Papers and broken dishware covered the floor. The only thing still on the counters in the kitchen were the microwave and fancy coffeemaker. The cabinets were open and empty. The refrigerator had been opened and emptied, including the leftover chili he had planned to serve tonight. "What a mess!"

"It's bad upstairs too." Bobby entered the kitchen then turned away. "I don't think Miss Dorie will like what happened in her bedroom."

Ross took the stairs two at a time. Star was okay in her crate, praise God. The drawers had been dumped, the closet ransacked, and the pillows slit open. His heart sank. Everything Dorie had brought to this room was likely ruined. She didn't need to see this mess. Now they all needed to shop for clothes between this and the fire at Riley's house that burned it to the ground.

He left the bedroom and walked down the hall. The attic landing door was open. He took the steps to the attic. The cedar chests were overturned with contents strewn over the floor. Until he and Riley figured out who was behind this assault, Dorie wasn't safe in this house. He pulled out his phone and called her.

"Hello, Ross?" It sounded like she was on the highway. "We're on our way back."

"You sound cheery. Did you find what you wanted?"

"All I need are shoes. They even had a veil like Grandma MacAvoy's. They're going to sew the pearls onto it for me."

Ross smiled. "Do you have the dresses with you?"

"Yes. Mine and Angela's red dress."

"On your way home, stop at Ethan's house and leave them in their house for safekeeping."

"Silly man, use some self-control to keep from looking at it."

Giggles from the three women filled his ear. Of course, he was on speakerphone through the car. He should have known.

"The house has been ransacked. Nearly everything is ruined, even the food in the fridge."

The women went silent. All he could hear was road noise.

Dorie finally answered him. "Okay, I can do that. What are you and Star going to do?"

"Riley can bring Star to you with her crate and food. Sweetheart, until we know what's going on and stop it, it's safer for you to stay in Daelin with Ethan and Lilah."

"What about you?" The plea in her request came straight through the air to Ross's heart.

"I need to clean up this mess and change the locks. And install a deadbolt on the inside of the second-floor attic door."

"Let me help." Her voice was small. He could barely hear it over the road noise.

"Okay, drop the dresses at Ethan's, inside the house. Then come on up. We'll figure it out from there."

"Who would do such a thing?" Angela's voice this time. "You two are loved by everybody. Who would try to hurt you?"

"Don't know. Make sure Dorie's okay to drive, Angie."

"Got it."

"Ross, I'll be there in an hour. I love you." Dorie's voice.

"I love you too. Drive safely. Try not to worry. Let Angela drive if you feel too agitated."

"See you soon."

"Ditto."

Ross hung up, his heart in a vise grip. He'd hoped he could clean up before she arrived. He walked down the stairs to join Bobby and Riley, to get their professional opinion.

"I'd suggest you guys go get new locks and dead

bolts while my detectives look over the scene, get some fingerprints, and any other evidence. I wouldn't sleep here tonight. I'll put a man on surveillance in case the person returns."

Ross stuck out his hand. "Thanks, Bobby. We'll get those new locks now."

DIANE E. TATUM

Chapter 13

Cleaning up the house …

Dorie arrived as Ross was installing a deadbolt on the front door.

"I left everything at Ethan's. It's bad, isn't it?" Dorie stood on tiptoes and put her arms around his neck. "I guess it's a good thing I took the pearls and veil with me."

"Yes, it is." He swung her up in his arms. "But I will keep you safe."

"You know who it is, don't you?" Dorie kissed him. "It's the same person who ruined your birthday party."

Ross nodded. "I'm afraid it is, but I don't understand how it could be. Riley's going to check it out." He sat down in a rocker on the porch and settled her into his lap. "It was my mom who killed everyone but my grandpa. She was sentenced to an institution for the criminally insane twenty plus years ago. I relegated her to the grave long ago. Guess I was wrong."

Dorie leaned against him, soaking in his warmth on this crisp December afternoon, dappled sunlight playing in the leaves, a light breeze stirring the brown leaves in the front yard.

"You don't think I'm safe here." It wasn't a question, just a statement of fact. "She sent me flowers, Ross. Maybe she's okay with me."

"I won't take that chance with you. Go up and sort through your things. When you see our room, you'll see what I mean."

Dorie extricated herself from his lap and arms. "It can't be that bad. We weren't even gone that long."

Ross sighed. "Come on." He took her hand and led her up the stairs.

Riley was at the end of the hall installing a deadbolt on the attic door. "Hey, Dorie. How went the wedding dress shopping? See anything you liked?"

"Yes, I bought a wonderful dress. Angie has a great looking red dress. I'd say it matched the tuxedo vest and tie I picked out, but I think I got outvoted." Dorie came to him and hugged him. "What did you guys do while all this mayhem happened?"

"I think I'm sworn to secrecy."

Dorie looked at Ross. "Yes, he is."

"Okay then." Dorie went to the bedroom door and looked in. A tornado would not have torn the room up as badly as the intruder had. "Oh, no." She sighed and sank down to the floor.

Ross squatted beside her. "Are you okay, love?"

"No. Vehemence is radiating from this disaster. Am I safe anywhere?" She looked into his eyes. "Are you?"

"That's why we're changing the locks and adding deadbolts." Riley came over and helped her up. "At least she didn't torch the house."

Ross stood. "That's not even funny. I'll get you a trash bag." He headed down the stairs.

"Is he okay?" She asked quietly. "I mean, this is a nightmare."

Riley shrugged. "I don't know. As long as he's busy, he's okay. What happens tonight when he tries to sleep? I can't say."

"He's going home with you tonight, isn't he?" Dorie couldn't imagine it.

"No, I'm staying here." Ross came up the steps and handed her a black yard bag. "The house should be secure by the time I'm here alone. Besides, she's my mom, if it's her. She didn't harm me before, she probably won't harm me now."

Dorie took the bag and entered to sort the damaged from the usable clothing. The usable she packed in a suitcase. She stripped the bed of the slashed sheets and pillowcases and remade the bed for Ross to use that night. They could pick up fresh pillows tomorrow. She gathered her toiletries from the bathroom and packed those as well.

She got the broom from the kitchen and swept the floors of the bedroom and upstairs hall of the fragments of clothing, boxes, and sawdust from the door drilling. When Dorie finished, Riley carried the suitcase down to her car.

"Leaving me already?" Ross grabbed her arm and turned her into a hug. "I'm not kidding. You didn't have to pack it all up."

"I don't need to be here. You're here. You should sleep in your own bed." Dorie kissed him. "I'll stay at Ethan's house with Star."

"I don't want you to go." Ross pouted like the little boy in the Beacon photograph.

Dorie touched his nose and kissed his cheek. "I know, but it's only three weeks until the wedding. After that, you won't be able to remove me from your home or your life. Frightening, isn't it?"

"Not at all. It will be heaven when I have you here with me forever." Ross kissed her deeply. "I guess it's less tempting this way."

"It will also deny the gossips a story to tell." Dorie held him close. "They won't be so concerned that we're 'living together' before the wedding."

Riley walked in the front door then closed and bolted it. "I doubt that. The gossips can find grist for the mill out of anything."

"How's the attic? Do you need help up there too?" Dorie looked from one to the other. "It's just as bad up there too, isn't it?"

"Worse." Ross finally found his voice. "But no one's trying to live up there."

"Are you sure about that? The shoplifted items included a lantern and a sleeping bag. I've been hearing sounds in the attic since before Thanksgiving. If the homeless lady is your mom, where else would she live? Especially after it got cold."

The three of them tromped up the wooden stairs to the attic. The attic was a mess before this event, but now the two cedar chests had been dumped over. All the contents were strewn over the attic. Ross and Riley turned them back over. Dorie helped gather the things she knew went in the MacAvoy chest, and Ross returned the Ross items to that chest.

Riley gathered up any trash and broken things. "Dorie, do you remember those shoplifted items? Do these items look like them?"

Dorie joined Riley at the cubby under the roof. "Sleeping bag, lantern, backpack. Yes, these are similar to items stolen from stores in Daelin. Ross, are these yours?"

"I honestly couldn't tell you if they've been here or not." Ross slumped onto the top of a chest. "This is the part of the rehab I've not paid any attention to. I can't say what was here or not."

"We could fingerprint the lantern." Riley used a rag to pick it up.

"That might not be definitive. I don't know how many people could have touched it or when. I've probably moved it when I've been up here. Dorie may have moved it too." Ross shrugged. "If you're looking for my mom's prints, they could be there too from twenty years ago."

Dorie looked out the window. The December sunlight had faded outside. "Are the locks all changed? We should finish, lock up, and get something to eat. Then we should all go to Daelin. That's what Bobby, the cop, said, right?"

"Yes, that's what he said, and I concur." Riley patted Ross on the back. "We've all been to Atlanta, sustained a shock, and worked hard to clean up. We all need a good night's sleep."

"But the house ..."

"Ross, darling, Bobby said they'd post surveillance tonight." Dorie sat beside him on the chest. "The new locks should keep everyone but us out. Bring all the keys from the locksets with us, so there's no chance of one falling into someone else's hands." She held his hand. "Your stuff is at Riley's place anyway."

"Are there any valuables stashed here that you need to take with you?" Riley finished the sweeping and closed the trash bag he'd been using.

"Grandpa's coin collection and medals from the war. There's a jewelry box somewhere. I don't know that anything in there is valuable, though." Ross turned to Dorie with exhausted eyes. You had the pearls with you. Did you leave them at Ethan's too?"

"Yes. I packed all of what's left of my stuff, including my memory box of Elliott and the ring." Dorie hated to bring up her late fiancé at such a distressing time.

"A good point. I wonder if your wedding ring is still here." The ring was part of a set his Grandma MacAvoy had worn. Dorie wore the engagement ring from the set.

Ross rushed down the attic stairs to the second-floor landing with Riley and Dorie behind him. He opened the bottom drawer of the bureau and stuck his hand to the back corner of the drawer. Then he withdrew the old velvet box and flipped it open. The ring was still there.

Dorie exhaled though she hadn't realized she'd been holding her breath. "I guess the intruder didn't take anything, as far as I can see. He or she just threw a temper tantrum and made a huge mess." Dorie took the box from Ross's hand. "Do you want me to add this to the wedding stuff stash at Ethan's house?"

"Probably should. We bought some wedding stuff too. It ought to be okay at Riley's." Ross winked at Dorie. "Some things will remain a mystery."

Dorie smiled but looked back to the dresser drawer. It seemed thicker than what appeared in the drawer itself. Was there a false bottom? She would have to check that out during her next time here.

"I'll go see if all the locks are locked and the deadbolts in place." Riley left them alone in the bedroom. "I'll meet y'all at the cars."

After Riley left, Ross put his arms around her waist. "We're in the bedroom alone."

Dorie laughed. "Not our wedding night yet. Don't get too excited."

"No, not tonight. Guess nobody's sleeping here tonight. We need to find out who's breaking into our house." Ross sighed. "I love you. Three weeks."

"Three weeks, Ross. I love you too." Dorie calmed herself. It didn't seem real, somehow, even though she'd bought the dress and veil. Christmas was coming too. She really wasn't ready for that either.

Chapter 14

Preparing for Christmas …

D orie woke in the cottage at Ethan and Lilah Andrews's home. She'd slept but still felt exhausted. She dragged herself from the bed and started a K-cup of coffee while she showered. She dressed, then let Star into Andrews's fenced back yard while she drank her coffee. The air was brisk. Were those snow flurries in the air? Aah, Christmas.

The thought of Christmas inspired terror in her heart. Not because of the wedding. Her family would be in Daelin/Helen for Christmas. That meant preparing a tree, buying gifts, planning places for them to stay, and planning meals that she wouldn't even be available to eat. If she and Ross were at The Doll House on Christmas Eve and on their honeymoon, wherever that would be, maybe her family could stay in Helen at their house. They could cook their own meals if she just bought the food for her three big brothers and parents.

"Dorie? You okay?"

Ethan jolted her out of her thoughts. "Yes, I'm fine. Just trying to think of all I need to do before

Christmas Eve." Dorie finished her coffee. "Come, Star. Time to go in and see Lilah."

Star took a lap of the yard at Greyhound Racer speed and dodged under the patio roof to the back door.

"Go on and finish getting ready. I'll take her in. I'll see you later." Ethan opened the French doors, and Star rushed into the house.

Dorie made sure to close the gate in the fence on her way back to the cottage at the end of the driveway. After finishing her preparations for the day, she drove herself to the Beacon office. She missed Ross. For so long, Ross had been the 'good morning' voice and a fresh cup of coffee for her. Abandoning their house seemed like abandoning each other.

The bells on the door jingled as Dorie entered the storefront office. The wind caught the door, causing her to drop her bag. She shoved her bangs out of her eyes, picked up her bag, fought the door again before getting into the office. Dorie struggled with her coat, lunch box and bag. She set up the laptop and went to the breakroom for more coffee.

Dorie started the coffee, since she was so early, and waited for the water to heat and run through the grounds. What gifts could she possibly get her parents and brothers? What would she get Ross or Riley? It seemed hopeless. When the steam rolled out at the last burst, she poured the coffee and turned around.

Into Ross's chest. Coffee splashed down his sweatshirt.

"I'm having déjà vu all over again, girl."

"Oh no, not again! What are you doing here?" Dorie scrambled to put down the mug of very hot coffee and find paper towels to clean up the mess.

Ross pulled off the sweatshirt. Only a small brown wet spot bloomed on his tee shirt. "I thought you were missing me as much as I was missing you. Do not pick up that cup before I hug you." He reached for her and snuggled into her neck and shoulder.

Dorie couldn't help laughing. Once she started, she couldn't stop. The stress that had built since the alarm had gone off dissipated. "I am the luckiest woman alive." She collapsed into his damp chest.

"That makes us well-matched and bodes well for the future. I know I fell in love with you when you threw coffee on me." Ross laughed. "You don't have to keep doing it, though."

Dorie broke into peals of laughter. Ross held onto her and laughed with her.

"Is there someone I can call?" Ethan and several other members of the Beacon were standing at the doorway watching them. "That honeymoon can't come soon enough. You guys need a vacation."

Dorie felt the hot blood rush into her face, and she buried it into Ross's chest.

Ross held her close. "You could be right, Ethan. But there's still three weeks until the wedding. Guess we'll hang in there until then."

Once their audience had dissipated, Dorie stretched to kiss him. "Sorry about the coffee. Where are we going on this honeymoon?"

"Ah, my love, that's a surprise." He hugged her and kissed her, then put his coffee-soaked sweatshirt on. "I think I need some clean clothes before I venture any farther. I'll catch up with you later."

As he headed out the door, he turned and called to her across the newsroom. "I forgot. I came to bring you breakfast. It's on your desk, including coffee."

Dorie waved to him before she bolted for the women's restroom. She closed the door and laughed out loud. When the giggles finally subsided, she checked her hair in the mirror. "We really are just cracking up, aren't we?" She nodded at her reflection, then went back to her desk to enjoy whatever Ross had brought her.

***

Ross headed up the mountain to check on the house. He couldn't believe Dorie had thrown coffee on him again, but the laughter that ensued was good for his soul. There was no doubt. She was his soulmate, his one true love, his one and only. No one had ever made him feel the way she did.

He pulled into the drive, in front of the house, next to the surveillance police car.

Ross rolled down his window. "So, how'd it go?"

"All quiet. We did see the security lights go on in the back, but we assumed it was just an animal." Bobby stretched in the police car. Then he got out and shook Ross's hand. "Want to take a walk around the property with me?"

"That's not necessary." Ross also stretched his back and shoulders. Riley's couch was going to kill him, he was sure of it.

"I'd just as soon take a walk around than leave and get a call to come back here."

Ross nodded. "Okay."

They walked the perimeter of the yard, then they checked the doors.

Bobby called Ross over to the garage door. It was unlocked.

"How?" Ross was flabbergasted. He knew they had locked every door.

"Some thieves are very clever." Bobby drew his gun. "Let's see if your visitor is still here."

Ross followed Bobby into the garage. The door to the attic was wide open, despite the locks. That was a lot of money and work down the drain. Good thing Dorie didn't sleep here last night. Wish I had though. I could have caught 'Goldilocks' in the act.

They climbed the stairs to the second floor. The door there had also been opened. Bobby pointed up the stairs with his gun. They climbed the second flight of stairs to the attic. It was dim in the early December light. Ross flipped the overhead light on.

The sleeping bag was freshly rolled and stashed someplace different. The lantern set up in a place to give light, not just be stored. The backpack was gone. This person had spent last night in the attic! This was proof positive.

"Someone spent the night here last night while you sat in your car outside." Ross worked to control his rage. What if Dorie had been here alone? Who was this person? "Should I call Daelin to get his crime scene detectives up here to dust for prints?"

And Ross had touched the light switch and ruined the best place for one. He shook his head at himself. If the suspect was his mom, she needed to stay far away from Dorie. He wouldn't have his future ruined by her like she had ruined his past.

"That's exactly what I'm going to do, Ross. We don't have the crime lab capability that Daelin does." Bobby held the cell phone to his ear. "Hi, this is Sgt. Bobby Bradford of Helen PD. We got another break-in at Ross MacAvoy's house and could use a visit from your crime scene boys … Sure, I'll wait… Captain McDonough, this is Sgt. Bobby Bradford of Helen PD. … Yes, I'm at Ross MacAvoy's. His visitor returned. We'd like help from your crime scene detectives. … No, sir. The new locks were no hindrance to this person. … Right, I'll tell him, sir. Thanks for your help."

Bobby hung up and faced Ross. "He said he's on his way with the crime scene boys. You should go back out with me and wait on him."

Ross nodded and headed back down the stairs. He tried not to touch the railing or the walls on the way down to the garage. He couldn't believe how easy the locks had failed him. He knew they took all the keys with them. Or had they?

Bobby followed him out to the cars.

Chapter 15

Determining a suspect …

D orie made notes as she researched what had happened to Ross's mom.

- Jeanine Ross MacAvoy pled guilty by reason of insanity in 1995 and was sentenced to the asylum for the criminally insane at Milledgeville, Georgia. Has a graveyard with bronze angel.
- Renamed Central State Hospital, it stopped accepting patients in 2010. Patients were moved into alternative facilities and into the community. 179 forensic (guilty by reason of insanity) patients remain in the Cook Building.
- Arrendale State Prison in Alto, Georgia, has mental health facilities for women.

It was precious little to work with. Before she started traveling to these sites, she'd talk to Riley first. Maybe the department had a file they'd let her view with a prisoner number, or history, or know a place to find out if she was still alive, incarcerated, and/or free.

Dorie packed her computer in her bag, grabbed her coat, and stuck her head in her editor's office. "Ethan, I'm headed over to PD to do some research on Ross's mom. Then I'll be staying in your cottage until the wedding, if that's okay. Ross called to say there'd been another break-in at our house." Our house. She liked the sound of that.

"You are welcome as long as you desire. Just stay safe. I worry that you like to live a little too close to the edge. I don't want to bury another reporter this year."

Trudy Jones was the reporter Dorie had replaced in May after graduation. Trudy had mysteriously disappeared. Dorie had found her decomposing body in a forest of kudzu.

"No worries, boss. I have a wedding to attend Christmas Eve." Dorie waved, then headed out. She left in her SUV so she could run up to the house if necessary.

Dorie entered Daelin Police Department and greeted the sergeant at the desk. "Hey, Joe, is the boss cop here?"

Joe grinned. "For you, he's always in."

That hot blood creep started up her throat. "Thanks, I'll find my way back, if that's okay."

"Anything for you, Miss Dorie." He waved her in past his big desk with the police blotter and phone.

Dorie hurried back to Riley's office. When she got there, Riley was in conference with someone she didn't know, so she waved at him and headed for the breakroom. She fixed a cup of coffee with Riley's new fancy coffee machine. She pulled out her laptop and searched multiple data bases for Jeanine Ross MacAvoy. Jeanine Annabelle Ross, Jeanine MacAvoy, Jeanine Ross. After all the permutations, Dorie had no luck.

She sipped her coffee. Then she tried a new search. Dorie searched for Ross's dad, Andrew Glen MacAvoy. She found a grim retelling of the birthday party and info about his gravesite. Still nothing about his murderer or her sentence. Google was clearly lacking info. She wondered if she could get hooked onto the station's secure web system.

Riley appeared at her elbow. Dorie hopped out of her chair and hugged him. He gave her a bear hug.

"This is a nice surprise, Dorie." Riley sat at the table with her. "What can I do for you?"

"I'm trying to find out what's happened to Ross's mom. I'm not having much luck though." Dorie showed him her notes. "What happened? It's like she's a phantom. I don't see much about the trial nor about her sentence or imprisonment."

Riley nodded. "What you're seeing is protection for Ross. The previous administration, especially before Google search and technology, tried to preserve the privacy of the victims of violent crime. Bet you didn't find much about Ross either."

"Not in regard to this event, no." Dorie sighed. "I get the desire to protect a five-year-old from the horrors of this crime, but what about his right to know?"

"He knows enough. I know enough about that day to last my lifetime." Riley stretched his arms over his head. "I know you want to know. Don't open this wound. It won't help Ross."

Dorie shook her head. "What if she's the person in our attic? What if she murders me in my sleep? Shouldn't we look for her before such a thing happens? What if she wants to finish Ross off?" She could feel her voice rising in anxiety. She knocked her coffee over and it soaked her yellow legal pad. "That's a second cup I've spilled today."

Riley jumped up and grabbed paper towels to soak up the spreading brown stain. "Relax, girl. Everything will be okay. Ross is at the house now. The police and detectives are checking for prints."

"Why? What's happened?" Dorie's anxiety jumped to alarm.

"Nothing. Whoever it was got in despite the locks and spent the night in the attic. Nobody's hurt, house is not damaged." Riley slid his chair over next to Dorie and wrapped an arm over her shoulder. "The crime scene detectives are there with Bobby from Helen PD. Ross is dealing with it. He just hasn't had time to call you yet."

Dorie covered her face with her hand. She had no desire to break down in Daelin PD's 'break room.' She probably wasn't the first to cry here. "The wedding is handled. Christmas and this intruder are killing me, Riley. Let me do this one thing. At least let me find out if she's alive or dead." She looked up at him.

Riley scratched his chin and looked into her eyes. "I've been thinking about something. You'll want to talk to Ross about it. You're such a good researcher. And you work well with the police. But Ethan would have to give you up."

"You're talking in riddles. Tell me what you're trying to say." Dorie wiped her eyes with one of the dry paper towels on the table. "What are you suggesting?"

"Working here, with us, instead of writing for the Beacon." Riley stopped and gave her a questioning look.

"Go ahead. Say it all." Dorie was surprisingly excited without even knowing what the job entailed.

"Investigative Communications Officer. You'd write our press releases, talk to the public, and use your investigative skills to help our detectives." Riley leaned forward. "What do you think?"

Dorie gasped. To work with Riley. No story deadlines. Would Ross be okay with it? He was a little jealous of Riley's attentions anyway. Ethan would not be happy, though. All these men and their egos. For that matter, her brothers. Perhaps it was time to do what she wanted to do. "Yes, I'll think on it and check with Ross. What about now? Can I snoop through your criminal database?"

Just then her phone rang. Ross. She put it on speaker after she answered it.

"Hey, Ross, I hear there's been a problem at our house again." Dorie continued questioning Riley with her eyes.

"Afraid so, my love. This is the first chance I've had to call you. How did you find out?"

"I'm sitting in Daelin PD with Riley, chasing down a lead. He just made me an interesting job offer." Dorie waited, holding her breath, for his reaction.

"What kind of job offer? Don't you have a job

already?"

Dorie detected a hint of irritation. Not a good sign. "Investigative Communications Officer."

"Really? What does that mean exactly?"

Yep, irritation. Even irked. "I would help with public relations, press releases, press conferences, and the detectives. What do you think?"

"Why?"

Dorie took a breath and blew it out slowly. "Riley thinks that since I do a fair amount of detective work that helps the police anyway, perhaps I could do it as part of my job."

The silence of the other end of the phone did not bode well. Finally, Ross responded. "How long have you been talking to Riley about this?"

"He just offered it to me now, right before the phone rang. Why are you unhappy? This could be a good thing." Dorie waited for his acquiescence because she realized he always gave her what she wanted. Maybe that wasn't fair. Perhaps she should give in sometimes.

"Will this mean you'll be a policeman? Will you have to go to the Academy? Will it change our wedding plans?" Ross paused. "If it's something you really want, I guess you'll do it anyway. I just don't want you in harm's way."

Riley shook his head. "It's not a full-fledged officer appointment. She won't have to go through police training. It's mostly a desk job with forays into the field to help detectives see from her investigative reporter perspective."

"Hello, Riley. I didn't realize this was a three-way conversation. Maybe Dorie and I should discuss

it between just us. I'll call you back later, Dorie."
Conversation ceased.

"I didn't realize he'd be so …" Riley seemed to be searching for words.

"Ticked off. Yeah, I figured that." Dorie put her phone back in the bag. "He's still jealous of you. He thinks you're trying to take me away from him. So, yeah, he's ticked off."

Dorie stewed for a moment or two. What to do? What to do? She pulled her phone back out of her bag and texted Ross. "Bringing lunch to the house. Do we need dishes?"

Immediate response said, "Buying some now. Should be back before you. Love you."

Relief washed over her. It would be okay.

"I'm headed to Helen, Riley. I'll have to let you know later about the job. I am interested, but not if Ross isn't happy about it." Dorie paused looking for a way to explain. "I'm marrying Ross. His opinion matters."

Riley nodded. "I get it. Let me know what the two of you decide."

On the way up the mountain, Dorie decided to stop for lunch to-go from Melody's Diner. She had an ulterior motive. When she opened the door, the bells chimed.

"Good morning!" came the chorus from the staff behind the counter.

Melody joined her at the counter where Dorie perched on a swivel bar chair. "How can I help you? Just about two weeks till the wedding, ain't it?"

Dorie nodded. "I need to place a to-go order. And I'd like to talk to Emmie while it's being fixed.

Is that okay?"

"Sure. Go sit at that corner booth, and I'll send Emmie out. What can I fix for you?"

Dorie ordered then went over to the indicated table. Emmie was a long-time friend of Ross's. In fact, she had wanted to marry him and go to college with him to have babies, at least that was Ross's version. Now she was engaged to Joe Morgan, the farmer north of town.

Emmie appeared immediately and took the other side bench.

"How can I help you?" Emmie fussed with her collar and apron, straightening it out.

Chapter 16

Beware the green-eyed monster …

Were you at Ross's fifth birthday party?"

Emmie's face flushed red. "Of course, I was. Ross, Riley, and me were the 'Three Musketeers' then. He could have five guests. The other three were Bobby Bradford, Jared Stanton, and Joe Morgan. We're all still rattling around this mountain, aren't we?"

Emmie's tone made Dorie feel like an outsider, which she guessed she was. Emmie also seemed angry. Not as friendly as other times they'd met. "What do you remember about it?"

"Well, it's about like remembering 9/11. I remember details about everything. His mom had on the cutest red check sundress with a little red shrug. She even had little red sandals. and her toenails and fingernails were painted the same shade of red. She was so pretty."

Dorie smiled. It was the first good thing she'd heard about Jeanine MacAvoy from that day. "And …"

"Ross's dad came in about the time to cut the cake. His mom was fixing drinks and using the ice pick on the ice from a grocery store. Then, he went over to kiss her, and she took the ice pick to his chest." Emmie had tears running down her face. "When his grandma cried out, his mom killed her too. Then his other grandparents were killed. Oh, Dorie, it was horrible. Blood was everywhere."

"I saw the photo of Ross from the paper." Dorie hoped she'd say something more.

"Ross grabbed onto his dad, that's whose blood is on Ross. She didn't ever try to kill Ross or any of the party guests." Emmie wiped her face and steeled herself. "We all shared a bond as a result."

"Of course, you would have to." Dorie felt a chill from Emmie's remark. "How are your wedding plans to Joe?"

"He broke our engagement." Emmie rubbed the finger that had previously held a ring. "He decided he couldn't make that commitment. Don't you think Mrs. MacAvoy killing her husband in front of five-year-olds created mental issues?"

Dorie felt her anger. "I'm sure it was traumatic, Emmie. Ross doesn't talk about it at all."

"You. Weren't. There."

The antagonism emanating from Emmie made her very happy to hear Melody call out that the order was ready. "Thanks for your information, Emmie. I value your friendship." Dorie scooted out of the booth and hurried to pay the bill and take the food on to Ross.

She climbed in the SUV and shivered from the cold reception she'd gotten from Emmie. Clearly, she shouldn't have asked. She hadn't realized that Joe and Bobby had also been there. Now Emmie had broken up with Joe, Bobby was a Helen cop and married with children, Jared had successfully saved her data from the computer Ryker had destroyed and was a newlywed, Ross was engaged to her, that left only Riley who shared this horrible bond. At least now she understood their attachment to one another.

She finally started the SUV and headed toward the house.

***

Ross was drying two new plates when Dorie's SUV pulled into the yard. He laid them on the table with the new tableware and napkins. Then he rushed to the door to be there and threw it open to greet her.

Dorie stepped into his arms. "I'm so sorry."

Ross was puzzled. "Why are you sorry? That's my line for distrusting you with Riley. At the end of the day, you'll still come home to me, right?"

"Of course, I would. It's primarily a desk job doing research on suspects." Dorie snuggled into his chest. "I'm marrying you in two and a half weeks."

"Then, you should take the job as long as Ethan is willing to let you go." Ross hugged her tightly. "What did you bring us for lunch?"

Dorie squirmed out of his embrace and took the takeout bag to the counter.

"Melody's? That's fantastic. I was expecting burgers and fries. What did you get?"

"Beef and barley soup with grilled ham and cheese sandwiches. Is that okay?" Dorie looked at him for approval.

Ross smiled back at her. "It's great. I love you, y'know?"

Ross helped Dorie with the cups of soup and sandwiches then got two cold cans of Coke out of the fridge. "This all smells so good. Did you run into Emmie there?"

Dorie sat in one of their new dining chairs. "Actually yes, but she was very angry."

"Hmmm. Let's pray." Ross took her hand and prayed a simple prayer of thanksgiving over the food. "Lord, thank you for my Dorie and for the food. Thank you for keeping us safe amid the break-ins. Help us to know Your will and to happily do it. Amen."

After a bite of sandwich, Ross turned to Dorie. "Why is Emmie angry?"

"Joe broke his engagement to her, and I asked about your fifth birthday party." Dorie looked penitent. "Yes, I've been doing research on the party and on your mother's whereabouts."

"Ah, I'm sorry to hear about Joe. Emmie's always thought she'd marry me. Perhaps that's why your presence angered her. That and the horrible memories you dredged up." He took another bite. He wasn't sure what else to say.

Dorie sat on the edge of the chair and grasped his hand. "Don't I have a right to know what happened to your family?"

"You have the right, my love, but must you dig all this up before the wedding?" He put down his spoon into the soup and used both hands to hold hers. "I love you. All I have is yours. Isn't that enough?"

"But what if it's your mom getting into the house, preparing to kill me?" Dorie came to tears. "What if she doesn't want me to have you? She killed all the adults around you."

Ross picked her up and put her in his lap. "Over

my dead body. I'm serious. No one is going to separate us from one another. That's what the wedding is about, you know. You and me, for eternity."

Dorie laid her head on his shoulder. "I know, but I'm afraid someone doesn't want our wedding to occur."

He held her close, felt her breath and her rapid heartbeat, and smelled the Hugo Boss for Women cologne on her. No one could replace her. No one would replace her if he had any word in the matter. He'd protect her with his life, if necessary.

"Our soup's getting cold." Dorie kissed his neck.

Ross chuckled. "I don't care. I'm not moving until you have no doubt of my love for you. You are the one and only wife I want."

"I want no other man. You don't need to be jealous of Riley." She snuggled into his neck. "It's just us in this relationship, right?"

"Absolutely." Ross's voice rumbled deep in his chest. He closed his eyes and shot a prayer heavenward. "Keep us safe and in each other's arms forever. Lord. Protect us from those who seek to harm us, divide us, or upset us. Give us assurance of each other's love. Let our bond and our promises grow stronger each day. Make us fit to serve you through our union. Amen."

Dorie whispered, "Amen."

"Are you okay to eat your lunch now?" Ross lifted her chin to look into her eyes.

She nodded, and he allowed her to leave the shelter of his arms. Then they finished their lunch from Melody's.

Chapter 17

Let the police handle it ...

Dorie helped Ross clear the dishes and dispose of trash from their lunch. "Guess I should go back to work."

"You could work from here, couldn't you?" Ross leaned against the counter and pulled her to him. "The view is better."

Dorie laughed. "For me or for you? No, I need to go talk to some people."

"Let the police do their job. You do yours." Ross kissed her. "I want you safe more than almost anything else. If you're not safe, I might not have the opportunity to marry you in two weeks."

"You are such a worrywart. You need to get back out in the forest, so you can think about other things." Dorie left his embrace and gathered her things together. "I will be fine. What could happen?"

Ross followed her to the door. "I can imagine many things."

She kissed him. "Don't worry. Are you staying at Riley's tonight?"

"I thought I'd stay here. I'm going to put some slide bolts on the doors to the attic and the outside, things that can't be manipulated from outside the house. Clearly the locks didn't keep someone out." Ross opened the door for her.

"I probably won't be back here tonight then. I've got work to finish." Dorie kissed him back. "Sleep well tonight."

***

When Dorie crossed into Daelin, she headed to Jared Stanton's computer shop. He had been able to retrieve her data from her damaged computer in October. To think, he was also one of those children at that ill-fated birthday party. Would he talk to her? Was the party really involved in the events of these past couple of weeks? Either way, it would be interesting to see what he had to say.

As Dorie opened the door to Computer Fix-It, a buzz went off in the shop. A man who must be Jared Stanton came from a curtained room behind the counter.

"How can I help you today?" He was shorter than Riley and Ross, but a cheerful-looking man. "Wait, I should know you. Aren't you Ross's Dorie?"

"Yes, his fiancée." Dorie felt a blush of satisfaction, Ross's Dorie had a nice ring to it.

"I'm Jared Stanton." He propped himself on a barstool behind the counter. "Another computer mishap?"

Dorie took a seat on a stool across the counter from him. "No, I wanted to ask you a couple questions about Ross and his birthday party. Emmie said you were there."

He ran his fingers through his thick brown hair

and frowned. "That's a topic I have been trying to forget for twenty-five years, Dorie."

"I understand that, but we're having some unusual events occur at the house that I'm afraid are related to that. I just need some perspective on that day."

Jared slid a bowl of Christmas candy to her. "Okay. I was excited that day to meet Ross's dad. Being a firefighter, he wasn't around as much as other dads were. We were five. He was a fireman! I couldn't wait for him to get to the party. I asked Mrs. MacAvoy when he was going to get there, probably one time to many. She seemed angry with me, so I stopped asking."

Jared carefully unwrapped the foil from a chocolate Christmas ball and popped it in his mouth. Dorie took a dark chocolate Hershey's Kiss from the bowl.

"You see," he continued, "I've thought what happened was somehow my fault. I shouldn't have kept asking her about him." Tears formed in his eyes. "But how could I, a five-year-old boy, have caused a grown woman to go over the edge?"

"Of course, it wasn't your fault." Dorie put the Kiss in her mouth to encourage him to talk.

"Mr. MacAvoy had on his turnout gear when he arrived, you know, to go along with the fire truck theme. None us ever got any of that firetruck cake. The worst part was Ross clinging to his dad and all the blood." Jared blinked. "I was afraid she was going to kill all of us. It's a wonder any of us is sane."

Dorie reached across the counter and took his hands in hers. "Thank you for telling me. Ross won't talk about it."

"They locked her up in a lunatic asylum in Milledgeville. Mama used to tell us 'If y'all don't behave, I'll send you to Milledgeville.' Worst threat she could make. Scared the bejesus out of us. 'Specially after they sent Ross's mom there. No way did I want to see her again."

Jared pulled his hands back. "I heard she was dead. I was always afraid she'd escape and come back for me." He shuddered. "Can I do anything else for you, Dorie?"

"Not right now. Thanks for extracting my data from my sick computer." Dorie gave him what she hoped was a comforting smile. "I'm sure I'll need your help again."

He nodded and returned to his work room behind the curtain.

Chapter 18

Driving to the asylum …

After Jared's stark description, Dorie headed to Java Joint. She needed to clear her head before pushing on to the inevitable trip to Milledgeville.

Angie greeted her with the regular call, "Mocha double shot. Chicken salad croissant?"

Dorie nodded and went back to the corner booth. She laughed when she saw the hand-lettered sign on the table: "Office of Dorie (Hudson) MacAvoy, Detective Extraordinaire."

"Like it?" Angie snuck up behind her. "Once you're married, I'm going to mount it."

"I love it." Dorie got out her computer while Angie put down her order. "I'm so glad we're friends."

"George is so excited about the red dress. He can't wait to take me to a New Year's Eve party." Angela sat down in the booth across from Dorie. "I love the dress. Thank you again."

Dorie smiled. "Glad I have at least one friend in Daelin."

"Now, hold on. There's …" Angie laughed.

"Riley's a guy and so is Ross."

"I've noticed." Dorie laughed. "You see the problem."

"Well, I'm married to a mechanic, and I spend my time pouring coffee to a majority clientele of men."

"I have three older brothers. You know I was always a tomboy hanging with the guys." Dorie sipped her mocha and yawned. "I guess I'm still hanging with the guys."

"I know the feeling. I've got three sons, you know. Sometimes it feels like testosterone poisoning and sweaty socks at my house." Angie yawned in response. "No fair yawning, I still got three hours left. Where's Ross tonight?"

"On the mountain. He's going to see if the intruder comes back after he adds a few new locks to the outer doors." Dorie bit an end off the croissant. "I wish he'd just stay with Riley for a couple more weeks. Then we'll be there together."

"I hear you. Men. They do what they want when they want."

The bell dinged at the counter.

"See you soon. Coming!" Angie jumped up and ran to get another order started.

Dorie brought up a Georgia traffic map to get directions to Milledgeville. Shame Ross wasn't going. Then she could say Ross had driven her to Milledgeville.

***

Dorie woke early and filed her article for the Daelin Beacon before heading to Java Joint for coffee and pastry to go. Then she drove over to

George's service station for gas, air in the tires, and a clean windshield. She waved good-bye to George and headed onto US 441 south to Milledgeville.

Two hours and thirty-nine minutes later, just as Google Maps had predicted, she crossed the town border, Milledgeville, Population 18,548. Antebellum homes and tree lined streets appeared before her as she turned off the highway into the town.

Signs directed her to Central State Hospital, clearly one of the biggest reasons for the town itself. When Dorie arrived at her destination, she saw one of those old historic markers: Georgia State Lunatic, Idiot, and Epileptic Asylum, founded 1842. Dorie wasn't sure what she'd find here, but no one else was willing to do the research for her or with her.

Dorie parked in the administration building lot. She got out of the SUV with the watery Coke she had picked up in Athens an hour or so ago. She stretched, finished the drink, then grabbed her bag with her computer, notepad, pens and pencils, and purse. Dorie climbed the steps into the ancient building in hopes of finding a place to start her search for Jeanine Annabelle Ross MacAvoy.

Dorie approached the receptionist desk. "Excuse me, I am looking for records of a prisoner admitted here in 1995. Can you point me in the right direction?"

The lady smiled a crooked smile and pointed at the cemetery visible out the window. "More than likely buried out there. No gravestones, and the markers aren't for specific graves either."

"What if she's still alive?" Dorie was shaken but

not wavering. She came for answers not a cold shoulder. "Where would I find records?"

The lady sighed. "Is this genealogy research? Trying to dig up weird old Aunt Emma?"

Dorie shook her head. "No. My fiancé's mother was an inmate here starting in 1995 and …"

"You want to invite her to the wedding?" The lady laughed out loud. "Sounds like a bad idea to me."

"Who is your superior? I'd like to speak to someone who's in charge." Dorie's pulse quickened as rage rushed through her blood. How dare she make light of anyone's relatives who had passed through those doors? "I'd like to see him or her now."

"Just a minute." She stabbed a button on the phone. "Mr. Anderson, there's a lady here looking for a former guest of Central State. … Yes, sir, I'll send her back." She took her time hanging up the phone. "When I buzz, the door will unlock for you. Ask for Mr. Anderson."

When Dorie reached the door, she heard the buzz and pushed her way into the main offices. Only a few people sat at desks scattered around the office. "I'm looking for Mr. Anderson."

A secretary-type person pointed to a large cubicle in the back corner.

Dorie crossed the office in a few steps and rapped on the door.

"Come in."

Dorie opened the door and saw a short older man putting a golf ball into a shot glass on the carpet.

"Are you the one who upset Jolene?" He shot the ball into the glass. "If I could only do that on the green, then I'd come up with more green at the end of a round. How can I help you?"

"I am trying to find out what happened to my fiancé's mother. She was sentenced to incarceration here in 1995. We're getting married soon, and we just want to know where she is or if she's passed away." Dorie struggled to be respectful while he continued to putt. "Any help you can give me would be wonderful. I did drive down from Helen today." Sorta.

"We went to a computerized system in 2015. You can see if she was transferred to Arrendale Prison." The golf ball rolled into the glass. "Aha! We have the old records in registries in the records office from before 2015. Twenty years is a long time in a mental institution."

He put his putter down and punched a button on his desk phone. "Yeah, Lydia. I got a lady here who needs access to our paper records and our computer info. I'll send her down to you."

Dorie threw her bag back up on her shoulder. "Where am I going?"

"You're going down that hallway you were in, then look for a door labeled 'Records Office'. Good luck with your search." Mr. Anderson prepared to shoot another putt.

Dorie had been dismissed. She wasn't too thrilled with the customer service. No one said a thing as she left the office and walked down the empty hall, her footsteps echoing. She finally found the Records Office door. She let herself in and stepped into an empty office. Dorie tapped on the counter with her keys. Then she rang the bell on the counter. When no one answered, Dorie stepped behind the counter and booted up the computer. She looked under the desk blotter and found a password which worked.

Dorie put in Jeanine Annabelle Ross MacAvoy. Nothing. Just MacAvoy. Nothing. Jeanine Ross. Nothing. Nothing. Nothing. Nothing. So much for hacking the data base.

"Can I help?" A lovely young woman appeared from nowhere.

Dorie jumped. "Sure. I'm looking for my fiancé's mother who was incarcerated here in 1995. My search brought up nothing."

"Well, then that means she wasn't here in 2015. Unfortunately, that means you must track her through the registries."

Dorie sighed. Maybe she should have booked a motel room.

"I'm Lydia. I can help."

"Do I need a motel room? I drove here from outside Helen, Georgia."

Lydia laughed. "Let's see how it goes. If we haven't found it by three, I'll recommend a good, inexpensive lodge for the night."

"Okay then."

Chapter 19

Dredging through mounds of paperwork …

Dorie followed Lydia into a musty, dusty room stacked high with registry books and filing cabinets. Little natural light filtered into the room. The neon tubes were harsh but necessary.

Lydia went straight to the stacks of books and pulled one. "This would be 1995 registry. You should be able to find her admission in here." She handed Dorie the book. "I'll start with 1999 for any mentions of her. Name?"

"Jeanine Annabelle Ross MacAvoy."

Dorie flipped open the 1995 book. It would be after Ross's birthday, May 20. How fast did the wheels of justice turn? Guess she'd have to go page by page from May 20. Dust escaped the pages probably never opened since 1995. Finally, she found it.

"Here it is, August 22, 1995. Jeanine MacAvoy admitted. Not guilty by reason of insanity for murder of four adults at children's birthday party." What followed was a list of medications to be administered with the dose and time of delivery. Room number 20 and building name was there. Dorie took a picture of the page with her phone and typed the info into her computer.

"Keep looking through the registries. She should be listed every time meds were changed or if she visited the infirmary, had a procedure, or had group therapy."

Dorie looked at the stack of volumes of years of registries. "Did they not keep files for each person?"

Lydia shrugged. "Of course. The chances of finding the file are incredibly low though. You can smell there's been water damage as well as see the upheaval when they were shifting patients to other facilities and digitizing info in 2015."

"So, going through the registries is recreating the file that should be here somewhere." Dorie sighed.

"Unless she was moved to another facility, in which case, the file would have moved with her." Lydia smiled. "It's not an impossible task, but it will take some time. I can look for the file, or I can help you look through the registries."

"I suppose taking the registries to a hotel room is out of the question?" Dorie began to feel claustrophobic in the musty records room, piled with paper and old record books.

"No, as long as you don't take them out of Milledgeville, I don't care. Don't tell anyone in Administration." Lydia started a stack of twenty registries. "I'll go get you a reservation at a lodge."

Dorie rested her head in her hands. The task was overwhelming. No wonder no one was willing to help. Her phone rang with the "Coffee House Jazz."

Ross.

"Hello, sweetheart."

"How's it going? I'm assuming you are in Milledgeville still." She could hear the fancy coffeemaker grinding beans in the background. "Find anything?"

"I've gone down the rabbit hole. I'm going to meet the Cheshire cat shortly with the Queen of Hearts right behind."

"Ah, darling. Surely there's a better way."

"The only way to find out anything about your mother is to plow through twenty years of record books. She's not in the digital records here. So, she either was transferred before that or died here." Dorie sneezed at the dust as she opened another book. "The records clerk is getting me a room for tonight at a lodge. It should be more comfortable than being on site."

"You know, every kid in Georgia was threatened with being sent to Milledgeville when they were bad. Except for me. Milledgeville was incredibly real to me and I knew I didn't want to go there. Grandpa knew that."

She heard him slurp coffee. "I wish I was there with you with a cup of coffee."

"Is it truly haunted? You know tourists go there in hopes of meeting a psycho ghost."

Dorie shuddered. "That's the last thing I'd like to encounter here. The clerk is coming back. I'm going to transfer this lot of books to a hotel room. Call you later, love."

"I love you. Good luck."

Lydia entered the room with a piece of paper.

"This is your reservation and a voucher for the night's room and meals tonight and tomorrow morning. As far as I'm concerned, you are doing research for the Hospital's benefit. You'll give me a copy of what you find, right?"

Dorie stared at the voucher. "Of course."

"Let me get a cart to move all those books. I also asked for someone to help you get them safely from your car to the room and back. They're primary documents. It'd be a shame to have them disappear or be ruined by a little rain." Lydia brought a cart in seconds later and began loading the bulky registries onto it.

Dorie packed up her things and helped Lydia with the record books.

"I'm going to go through some old filing cabinets looking for Mrs. MacAvoy's file. I'll let you know if I find anything. I'll copy it, so you can take it with you."

"You have been immensely helpful. How can I repay you?" Dorie helped her move the heavy cart down the stairs to her car.

"When you come back in the morning, bring me a mocha latte, two shots."

Dorie nearly dropped her end of the cart. "That's my drink too! Where do you get it?"

"I knew we were connecting on more than one wavelength! There's a coffee shop near the lodge. You can't miss it."

The two ladies loaded the volumes into the SUV.

"Good luck, Dorie. I hope you find what you're looking for." Lydia gave her a hug. "Congrats on your wedding."

"Thanks. I'll see you in the morning with a mocha double shot latte."

Dorie climbed in and followed the directions to a quaint bed and breakfast called the Antebellum Inn. While she registered, two young men carried the books to her room. The receptionist showed her to her room for the night.

What a room! She had expected EconoInn. Instead she had a four-poster queen bed, a lounging couch, a desk and chair, Wi-Fi, and a beautiful view of manicured lawns and flower beds, gazebos, and swings. Of course, it was winter, but Dorie had a good imagination of what it would be like in summer. Maybe Ross and she could come here... Where was her head? Ross never needed to come to Milledgeville, especially for vacation.

She freshened up and wished she'd brought an overnight bag.

Chapter 20

How the intruder entered the house …

While Dorie was on her fishing expedition in Milledgeville, Ross set about preparing the other three bedrooms in the house for company. Dorie's family planned to stay there December 23-25 for the wedding festivities. The junk needed to be trashed or moved to the attic. Then he needed two more beds, maybe a sleeper sofa for the third room as an office for Dorie. Should he stay at Riley's or bunk on the futon, again? Futon again, he suspected. He'd be a poor host to not be here to take care of their guests. He wanted Dorie in Daelin away from whatever craziness was going on in the attic.

He cleaned windows, vacuumed, and completed some wood trim he'd left undone when he left for California. Then he headed to Melody's Diner to meet Riley for lunch.

Ross got there before Riley, so he grabbed a booth when one was available and waited.

"Good afternoon, Ross." Emmie greeted him as usual. "What can I get for you today?"

"A Coke and a burger plate."

"Where's your fiancée, Miss Dorie?"

"She's doing research near Macon today. Riley's going to be here soon." The bell on the door jangled. "There he is now. Why don't you wait and get his order too?"

"How's the wedding plans?"

She seemed edgy to Ross. "They're going just fine. The Doll House is our venue, Pastor is the officiant, flowers from Marjorie's, and invitations by Jared. Are you planning to come on Christmas Eve?"

"I'm not sure if I can, Ross. After all it is Christmas Eve."

Riley approached the table and sat down. "How are you doing, Emmie?"

"I'm okay. Are you happy with Dorie stickin' her nose into this birthday party thing?" She gave Ross a sour look with her question. "I mean, what good can come from diggin' up stuff that should stay buried, includin' your momma?"

"Wow! That's a little harsh, don't you think, Emmie?" Riley took her hand. "What's eatin' you?"

"Nothing. I'm just doin' my job. What are you eatin'?" Emmie flinched away from Riley.

"What's Ross having?" Riley scanned the menu.

"Burger plate and a Coke." Emmie tapped her receipt book with her pencil.

"I'll have that too." Riley reached for her hand again. "What's wrong?"

"Nothing. Just sight, unseen, if you know what I mean." Emmie jerked away from him. "I'll just get your order in and pour your Cokes."

Riley looked at Ross, who held up his hands in surrender.

"I have no idea what that was about." Ross grabbed a napkin out of the dispenser on the table. "Seems to be about Dorie doing research on what happened to my mother."

"Sure it's not more than that?" Riley got a napkin too. "Emmie was your high school sweetheart, you know."

"And I broke it off when she wanted to get married, come to college with me, and have babies. That's been over ten years ago. Ancient history." Ross salted his napkin so the sweating glass wouldn't stick to it.

Emmie brought their drinks then left without saying a word.

"You're moving on, but she's still doing the same job she did in high school. Maybe she thought you'd come back to her someday." Riley sipped the soda. "She's a good woman. Did you never think of her again?"

Ross blew a straw wrapper across the table at Riley. "Of course. But Grandpa was suddenly dead too. I felt dead inside. Too much death for a twenty-two-year-old to handle."

"So, what's so different about Dorie?" Riley threw the straw wrapper back at him.

Ross shook his head. "I don't know how to describe it. The day we met, when she threw coffee on my fresh church shirt and tie, something inside of me knew, just knew, she was the one I was waiting for. The one who could help me live again after so much death."

"Then you almost lost her." Riley sat back as Melody delivered their burgers.

"What happened to our waitress?" Ross took the plate from Melody.

"I don't know. Emmie hadn't been the same since you and Dorie got engaged and she and Joe broke up. Can I get you anything else, boys?"

"Ketchup." All three stated in unison,

"I'll go get you a bottle." Melody turned and headed back to the counter.

Melody returned with the ketchup. "By the way, do I need to care for Star while you are gone during Christmas."

"No, she's staying down in Daelin with Ethan and Lilah Andrews. Oh, you need new keys to my place. We changed the locks after some funny business." Ross reached in his pocket for a set. "Just pitch the old keys and put these on the old keyring."

"No problem. When is Dorie getting back?"

"Hopefully tomorrow. We have invitations to deliver." Ross grinned what he figured must be a sappy grin. He couldn't help it though. Dorie was going to marry him. Would anyone chew him out for being happy? He didn't think so, and anyone who would, could take a flying leap.

Melody came back with their check a few minutes later. "Ross, I don't know how to tell you this, …" She stood by the table, twisting her apron hem.

"What is it?" Ross couldn't imagine Melody with nothing to say. "Just say it, you know, like ripping off the Band-aid."

"The old keys are missing from the register." Melody slid in next to Riley. "I don't know who would take them or how they'd get them. I stash them in the register instead of hanging them where anybody could grab them."

"Who has access to the register?" Riley took over the conversation while Ross processed the info.

Melody grabbed one of Ross's hands. "Well, just the girls and me. The cooks never have a reason. Oh, Ross, did I allow that 'funny business' you were talkin' about?"

Ross finally cleared the mind fog. "Don't you worry about it, Melody. Have you had any break-ins?"

"No." Melody began to tear up. "I am so sorry."

"I insisted Dorie move back to Daelin to Ethan Andrews' cottage to get her out of the house. I'm going to be there till the wedding. After that, I'll be there with Dorie."

"Here, take these keys. I don't want to hurt you both again."

As Ross reached for the keys, Riley stopped him.

"No, put the keys back in the register. Whoever took them knows the old ones are no good." Riley closed Melody's hand on the keys. "When they use them, we'll catch them."

Melody's tears spilled onto her cheeks. "Who do you think would do such a thing? You think it was Emmie?"

"No!" Ross couldn't think that of Emmie. "There's a homeless woman in Daelin we think is camping in my attic. She stole my credit card. She may have been here and got her hand in the drawer while no one was looking." Ross handed Melody a napkin from the dispenser.

Melody wiped her tears. "I'll keep a lookout on the register. I'm so sorry, Ross."

"It's okay. No one's been hurt." Riley took the check. "Show me the register and how it works."

Ross reached for his wallet.

Riley waved him off. "Let me get this today. You can pay another day."

Ross followed them to the register.

Riley looked into the cash drawer and how the register worked. Then he paid their tab.

Both men exited the diner. The wind on the mountain had picked up strength and coldness.

"Christmas is getting close, Ross. Guess you're gaining a wife and losing your freedom for Christmas." Riley laughed.

"Gaining Dorie is gaining freedom, from a certain way of thinking." Ross opened the door to Grandpa's old truck. "You should know that. You love her too." Ross elbowed him in the ribs.

"Got it." Riley moved to avoid another jab.

"You know what really bothers me though? I swore to Dorie that she and I had the only sets of keys. We both forgot the ones Melody used to let the dog out."

Riley leaned against the truck. "I'm surprised Dorie hasn't thought of that. If she were here, she'd know who was using those keys."

"She's on the track of a different crime. No wonder her head's not in this mystery." Ross stuck his hands in the pockets of his forest ranger wool coat. "That wind is cold. I better get back to the house. I ordered some furniture that's arriving today."

He and Riley bear hugged.

"I'm going in search of the homeless woman. She may know something." Riley climbed into his police service vehicle and headed down the mountain road to Daelin.

Ross waved then got in the truck. He headed for home. There was still much to do before the rehearsal dinner and the arrival of their guests from St. Louis.

DIANE E. TATUM

Chapter 21

Learning more about Ross's mom ...

Dorie spent most of the night going through registries from Central State Hospital. A pity since the four-poster bed looked so inviting. Her neck and head ached, but she figured it was a labor of love for Ross. He needed to know what became of his mom before he moved on to a new life with her. She needed to know if the mysterious visitor to the attic was Ross's mom.

It was nigh on three AM when she reached the concluding entry: May 20, 2008. Jeanine MacAvoy, found dead in room 20 from self-administered prescription medicine. Buried in Cedar Lane Cemetery.

Jeanine took her own life on Ross's eighteenth birthday. The staff was probably baffled at why that particular day. It was also thirteen years since the murders at the ill-fated birthday party for precious five-year-old Ross. Tears ran down Dorie's face. Over the twelve hours she'd spent examining the registries, transcribing the day to day rituals of her life, Dorie felt she'd come to understand her pain as well as her disease.

Jeanine had been lucid in many ways. She planned the suicide while the help the meds would have given her in the two weeks prior to her death vanished. She remembered her little boy. She knew the pain she'd caused him. She loved him, and in her way, did the only thing that she could do to help him survive the upside-down world she had lived in.

Dorie finished documenting the final entry and saving it all on her computer. She stacked all the registries for removal to her car in a few hours. Then she laid in the luxurious bed, fully clothed, until her cell phone alarm went off at eight, breakfast time at the Antebellum Inn.

After freshening up as best she could, Dorie went down to breakfast, then she visited a flower shop, purchased a bridal bouquet, and the local coffee shop where she bought two double shot mochas.

Lydia met her on the steps of Central State. Two young men waited with a cart and wrestled the registries from her SUV, onto the cart, up the steps, and into the building.

"Success?" Lydia gladly accepted the coffee cup from Dorie and took a sip.

"Yes, she committed suicide May 20, 2008, Ross's eighteenth birthday." Dorie sipped from her cup. "It was all so sad. How would you like the information I dug out? I can email a file to you, or I can come in and print a copy."

"More paper? No thanks. Send me the digital file. I can then load it into the database." Lydia took a long drink from the cup. "Did it say where she's buried?"

"Cedar Lane Cemetery. I'm headed there next."

Lydia smiled. "You know those graves are not marked."

"Something I saw online suggested that the markers had been pulled up by overly ambitious volunteers." Dorie took another sip. "It's okay. I have a plan. Thanks for all your help, the dinner voucher, the room, breakfast, and the liberty to be alone with your precious registries."

"I wish we had the manpower to do the exact same thing for every resident of this place from the beginning before the records are destroyed by age, water, or vermin."

"Thanks. It's a gift I can give her son, whenever he decides he wants to know." Dorie climbed back in the SUV, out of the cold breeze. "I'll send the file when I get back to Helen."

Lydia waved and turned to go back to her office, sipping her mocha latte as she went.

Dorie steered the SUV around the corner and down the block until she reached the Cedar Lane Cemetery. Iron stakes were driven into the ground at regular intervals. A sculpture of an angel welcomed Dorie to the solemn resting place of too many who were victims of diseases of the mind. She wiped away her tears and stepped out of the car with the bridal bouquet the florist had created for her that morning. She walked to the angel and placed the bouquet in her hand. Using florist wire, she secured the flowers so they wouldn't blow away before they froze or wilted.

"Lord, bless this place and care for your children, afflicted with diseases that were misunderstood causing them shame and isolation from society. Help them to be remembered even though their individual grave is unmarked. Bring them peace they never knew in life. Amen."

Dorie wiped away her tears. Then she headed back to Ross to share what she'd learned with him in Helen.

***

Riley drove slowly down the alleyways and back streets where the homeless tended to congregate, even on a cold day like this, so close to Christmas. Occasionally he'd stop and show the picture of the homeless lady to someone. Most shook their heads, thinking they were helping her escape arrest. At this point, Riley just wanted to know who she was and if she bore Dorie any harm.

Ross was right. He was in love with Dorie. Riley knew Dorie loved Ross and would marry him in a little over a week. He wouldn't do anything to stop that, he loved them both too much to cause them pain. Someday he'd find his own Dorie, though he had doubts about how that could happen. Ross was also right, Emmie was not the same as Dorie. Joe shouldn't have dumped her, but Riley had never been interested in Emmie. She was always Ross's girl, from kindergarten until graduation from high school.

Then he saw the homeless woman from the artist rendering. She was huddled around a fire in a barrel with several other disheveled people. Riley carefully got out of the chief's vehicle and approached the group.

"Cold out here?" Riley joined the group around the fire.

Murmurs acknowledged his presence.

"You should know that the mission is open and has beds for these cold nights."

"Gotcha Chief Riley." One of the younger men had answered him. "Most of us don't want what they're selling down there at the mission."

"That's right. Like Jesus is gonna do a miracle and give us a nice warm home with the money to keep it." The second man laughed. "No thanks. Ain't seen no miracle like that, no how."

"You don't have to believe to keep from freezing though." Riley warmed his hands at the fire with them. "I don't want to see any of you die from too much pride. Understand what I mean?"

Murmurs answered him.

Riley looked at the lady from the sketch. "Some folks around town think they may know you. What's your name?"

"Don't want no trouble with the cops, Chief." She backed away from him.

"No trouble, no trouble. I'm just trying to clear up a mystery, ma'am." Riley backed up from her. "It's a small matter that I can clear up in a short time. Maybe over dinner at the café on the corner."

"Whoa, Sally. You done got yourself a suitor!" One of the men laughed while the other hooted.

"Just some talk for a hot meal and coffee?" Sally stepped closer.

"Yep. That's the deal. And I'll take you to the women's shelter for a warm night's rest in the bargain."

"Not the lockup?" Sally drew closer.

"No. You ask the guys. I deal fair, don't I?"

Riley held his hands up. "No tricks."

"Not like that guy that covered up that murder over the summer." One of the men nodded. "You can trust ol' Riley here."

The other man nodded.

"Ok. I'll take you at your word, Chief."

The corner café was nothing special, but the food was hot and good. Riley led Sally to his favorite table and ordered two coffees on his way to the booth.

Sally scooted into the booth.

In the glare of the neon, Riley could tell she might be younger that anyone might think she was. No way was she Mrs. MacAvoy. He handed her the menu as the waitress placed the coffee on the table.

"What can I get you and your lovely lady tonight?" The waitress wore a checked apron and a nametag that read 'Jenny.'

Sally blushed. "Now, don't you put no lipstick on a pig, ma'am. I know I don't look good enough to be here. I just appreciate your kindness for not kicking me out."

"Jenny, I'd like your Salisbury steak with mashed taters and green beans. What looks good, Sally?" Riley poked at her menu. "This is what I'm getting. The fried chicken is good, too. Don't worry about the prices. It's my treat, remember?"

"Fried chicken would hit the spot with taters and beans, too."

"I'll bring it right out." Jenny winked at Riley before she left.

"Oh, she's sweet on you, Chief Riley. I can see

why. You're kind as well as handsome. That don't come often together, y'know?"

Riley felt himself blushing. "Ah now, don't put no lipstick on a pig, to quote you."

"I ain't kiddin'. You are kind and handsome."

"Where you from, Sally?" He sipped his black coffee, not as good as Java Joint, but hot.

"Originally from here. Then after what happened, I got out of town before everyone started blamin' me." She seemed raw. "I caused it all, y'see."

"What did you cause?" Riley was confused, but clearly Sally had a story to tell.

"All those murders. In front of all those babies. It was awful, and it was my fault." She wiped a tear that left a smudge on her skin.

"Are you talking about the birthday party murders?" Riley couldn't believe his ears. "That was twenty-five years ago, Sally."

"Don't mean it don't still matter." Sally dumped sugar and cream in her coffee and gave it a vigorous stir.

"I was at that party, Sally. I don't remember you being there or involved in any way." Riley took another sip. Sometimes these folks were out of their heads.

"I was having an affair with the fireman, Glen MacAvoy. His wife found out and killed every adult at that party."

Chapter 22

Seeing a new perspective …

Riley worked hard at keeping his mouth closed. He wanted to yell, "What?" but she'd stopped talking then. "Glen MacAvoy? You had an affair with Ross MacAvoy's dad?"

"Not proud of it, mind you." She sipped her coffee.

When the food arrived, Sally ate it like she'd not ever see food again. Riley could barely eat after her confession.

"I need to ask an extremely serious question, Sally. I need the truth." She nodded and he continued. "Have you been up in Helen since you've been back?"

"How am I going to get to Helen? Walk all that way in the cold? No, sir. I haven't been to Helen since twenty-five years ago. It was the last time I saw Glen. He was gonna leave her, and we were gonna raise his boy. Maybe have other children."

"So, what happened to you, Sally?"

"I got out of town. I wasn't gonna stick 'round and have her blame me for the murders. She was plum crazy. They locked her up, and she should stay locked up! Can I have dessert, too?"

Riley nodded and waved Jenny over. "Pie for the lady?"

"We got blueberry, raspberry, cherry, chocolate, and banana cream."

Sally looked like she'd glimpsed heaven. Pie should not receive such a response. She was another victim of Jeanine MacAvoy.

"Chocolate."

"Riley, you want a piece?" Jenny poised her pen over the order book.

Cherry was Dorie's favorite. Riley sighed. "Wrap a chocolate to go for me, Jenny."

"You got it. Two chocolate pies, one to go." She winked at him again.

"You need to ask that girl out, Chief. She's flirtin' with you."

Riley smiled at Sally. "You might be right. Once you eat your pie, I'll take you to the women'shelter."

"You know how to show a woman a good time, don'cha?" Then she laughed.

"Tell me about the flowers you sent Dorie and wrote Ross's name on."

"You know about that? I'm not supposed to tell about that."

"What happened? How did you know to send them to Dorie?" Riley was more perplexed all the time by this woman.

"Well, Ross gave me money, ten whole dollars. Wait, was that Glen's boy, Ross?"

"Yes, it was." Riley smiled. All the pieces were coming together in a way he'd never seen coming.

"Then his Grandpa MacAvoy did a good job

raising him. Handsome too, like his daddy now that I think on it. Dorie's his girl then, right?"

Yes, ma'am."

"Well, Ross had dropped his credit card out of his wallet. I saw it after he left me. I started to call out to him, but another girl stopped me. She said I could do him a favor with that card, and then it'd be mine to use as I liked." Sally frowned. "That wasn't true, was it?"

Riley shook his head.

"Anyway, I ordered the flowers with the message she said. The florist had no trouble with the card. I used it to get some essentials for winter. That's all. Just essentials."

"Who told you to do this floral delivery to Dorie?"

"I don't know her name. She's cute, kinda your age."

"Can you describe her to an artist, Sally?"

Jenny brought the pie then, and Sally enjoyed every bit of hers. Riley's was wrapped to go. She also brought him the check. On it, Jenny had written, "Call me". He looked up, and she had her thumb and finger to her ear and mouth. He nodded.

"Sure, I can." Sally interrupted Riley's flirtation with Jenny. "Describe her to an artist. You need to take that girl out."

Riley called the PD and asked the artist to meet them at the shelter. He paid the check with a generous tip.

"See you later, Riley." Jenny smiled.

Riley almost tripped over the threshold. Then he drove Sally to a shelter and helped get her settled for the night. She described the lady to the artist, but it was generic.

"See you later, Sally. Take care of yourself." Riley patted her on the back. "By the way, you saw Dorie, Ross's fiancée. She was putting flowers on the Ross and MacAvoy graves when you were visiting Glen MacAvoy's grave."

"She put the flowers I sent on their graves? She's a good girl, isn't she?"

"One of the best I've ever met." Riley felt that crimp in his heart. "Ross deserves a great wife. Dorie loves him."

"And you love her too, don'cha?" Sally grabbed his hand. "Don't worry. Jenny seems like a good girl, too."

"I'm sure you're right." Riley headed back to his townhouse.

***

Ross answered his phone. "Dorie, are you almost in Daelin?"

"Nope, I'm on your front lawn. I'll be in as soon as I get out with my computer. I have information about your mom."

"Well, come on in. It's your house, too."

Ross reached the front door in three strides and flung it open before Dorie could reach the front porch. He grabbed her and spun her around. "I missed you so much. What did you find out?"

Dorie stretched up to kiss him. Ross gathered her in his arms, and they kissed. He carried her to the couch, sat her down gently then sat beside her.

"How was the trip?" Ross put his arms around her. "I've never wanted to make that trip to

Milledgeville. I tried to remember the mom she was before that party."

"If you don't want the details, they can keep until another time, sweetheart." Dorie traced the line of his jaw with her hand.

Ross took her hand and shook his head. "No, I have you now. I should be able to handle the truth as long as you are at my side."

"First, your mother took her own life on your eighteenth birthday. She loved you all those years. She remembered you. The pain of what she'd done caused her to stop taking her meds and then she took them all on that day."

Ross felt like he would vomit. So much pain. So much loss. "So, she is dead."

He stood, leaving Dorie on the couch, and went to look out on the mountain. She wasn't the homeless lady who stole his credit card. She wasn't the lady visiting his father's grave. His mom had been dead since he'd graduated high school.

The pain in the pit of his stomach grew worse. He should have gone to see his mom. He should have forgiven her for taking away his grandparents and father. Ross knew he'd have to find a way to forgive her now, to forgive them all for leaving him too soon.

Dorie's arm slipped around his waist. "I'm so sorry, sweetheart. I can go if you need time to process it all. There's a paper file folder and a flash drive with everything I found out. I can head back to Daelin if you like."

"Before you go, let me show you what I've done while you were gone." He took her hand and led her upstairs.

When they reached the upstairs landing, the hall light came on.

"Motion detector. When guests are up looking for the hall bathroom, they can see where they're going even though they don't know where the light switch is."

Dorie squeezed his arm. "That's brilliant."

"I thought so. Bedroom #2 I call the Rose Bedroom." Ross turned on the light switch and a new lamp on the nightstand beside a new bed came on. "I even bought a pretty quilt with roses for the bed." The walls were a pale coral pink.

"I love it." Dorie raced to the next bedroom.

Ross turned on the light in Bedroom #3. "I call this the Spring Day Bedroom."

The sky-blue walls blended into a quilt of similar color with trees full of birds and flowers on the grassy lawn with butterflies.

"These rooms look wonderful." Dorie gushed. "You are amazing."

"Wait, one more room. Bedroom #4. I call it Dorie's Place." He flipped on the light.

The walls above a chair rail were a pale beige. Below the chair rail the wall was navy blue. A sofa sat against one wall, a desk with a fancy office chair was on the opposite wall.

"Oh my!" Dorie ran her hand over the old wood. "Did this come from the attic?"

"Yes. It took Riley and me forever to get it down those attic steps and into this room. If we ever sell the house, the desk goes with the house."

"No way. I love it. Did you have to refinish it?" Dorie sat in the desk chair.

"No, a little furniture polish and elbow grease restored the beauty of the wood. This is your office, darling. And the sofa is a pull-out bed for guests when needed."

Dorie stood and embraced him. "I love it all. You got a lot done while I was gone."

"Had to. Your family will be here in a week." Ross kissed the top of her head.

Dorie squeezed him tighter. "A week! Is it really only a week away?"

Ross led her to the sofa and sat, pulling her to him. "Just about a week until the festivities begin. Are you ready to be Dorie MacAvoy?"

"Yes. I guess we should hand deliver invitations. They'd never make it in time if we addressed and mailed them."

"Save that worry for another day, love. Why don't you go ahead to Daelin and get some sleep? I'll look over what you brought me then try to do the same." Ross gave her a long searching kiss. She'd better leave now. This is feeling too natural to continue if she stays. "You should go before I lose what's left of my control, girl."

Dorie's look echoed his own desire. "You're right. I should go." She got up from the sofa and finger combed her auburn curls into some manner of control.

Ross stood and followed her down the stairs. "How do you like my decorating?"

"You did a great job. I love you, and I've been praying for you while I've been gone." Dorie kissed him. "I left a bridal bouquet like the one I'll carry down the aisle tied to the bronze angel in the cemetery where your mom is buried. There are no headstones, or I'd have left it on her grave. The picture of the angel with the bouquet is on the flash drive, too."

"Ah, darling, you're an angel. Be safe on the mountain road." Ross let go of her with reluctance. "Sleep well, my love."

Dorie waved after she started the car. He waved back. When she was out of sight, Ross went in to look at what Dorie had found.

Ross sat on the sofa and opened the folder. Clipped to the left front was a picture of his beautiful mother, the one he remembered. That's when tears streamed down his face.

Chapter 23

Fitting the puzzle pieces together …

Dorie entered Java Joint for lunch. Angela greeted her by calling out her regular order. She took her seat in her regular booth. The sign Angela had created was mounted on the booth wall.

Angela brought her mocha double shot and chicken salad croissant. "How's the planning? The big day's just a week away. I can't wait."

"Well, I'm feeling nervous suddenly now it's so soon." Dorie sipped her coffee. "It seems like it's such a fuss for a commitment we've already made in our hearts."

"What did you find in Milledgeville? Ah, never mind. Tell me later."

The bells on the door jangled. Christmas lights around the shop twinkled. The tree in a corner glowed. When had it become Christmas?

Riley appeared at the table. "Morning, Dorie. You would not believe what I learned yesterday."

"I learned a lot in Milledgeville, too." Dorie stood and hugged him. "Ross should be here soon."

They both sat just as Angela brought Riley's

coffee and sandwich. "Ross coming too?"

The door jangled again.

"That's probably Ross." Angela ran off to fix his regular order.

Dorie jumped up and greeted him with an embrace and a kiss. Angela brought Ross's order. "Only a week until the big day, Ross. I can't wait."

"I can't wait until it's over!" Ross slid in next to Dorie. "Normalcy, that's what I'm looking forward to."

Dorie grabbed his hand and squeezed it. "I can agree with that."

"I found the homeless lady. Her name is Sally. She knew your parents, Ross."

"Really? Who is she?" Ross sipped his coffee. "Dorie found out my mom died on my eighteenth birthday. So, it's not my mom."

"Well, it's not Sally either. She said she wouldn't climb the mountain road in this cold." Riley took a bite of sandwich. "The crazy part is she said she was having an affair with your dad."

"What? That can't be true." Ross turned a shade of red.

Dorie grabbed his arm. "How do you know? You were five. As children, we think our parents are perfect. But clearly they were human like we are."

"Sally said she was the cause of your mom's breakdown." Riley reached across the table. "It's hard to know for sure, of course."

"Who gave Ross's credit card to Sally and told her to send me flowers then?" Dorie had the feeling Ross was going to fly away if she didn't hold on to him. It was too much to take in.

"She gave the artist a description, but the face is bland. Hard to know any details from it." Riley pulled a paper from his pocket. "She's younger than Sally or your mom. More our age, I guess." He handed it to Dorie.

Dorie wasn't sure, but she looked a little familiar. "I feel like I know her." She handed it to Ross. "What do you think?"

Ross looked at the paper. "It could be anyone. I'm going to Jared's to pick up the invitations. We got to get them to people if we want them to come." He kissed Dorie and left.

"Was it something I said?" Riley held Dorie's hand. "I think he's recognized her."

"Who do you think it is?" Dorie didn't know half the people Ross knew. She didn't really expect to know the woman in the sketch.

"I'd only be speculating. I need to get back." Riley stood. "Keep thinking about that job offer, okay?"

Dorie nodded.

Angela slid into the booth. "Everything okay? Ross looked like he could spit nails."

"I know. This pre-wedding stuff is getting harder. It's dredging up twenty-five-years-worth of family history. Most of it unhappy, I'm afraid. We haven't uncovered the mystery visitor in the attic yet." Dorie frowned. "I'm not surprised he's longing for days after the wedding."

"Don't be worried, Dorie. Ross loves you. You'll see. It will be okay."

Dorie stayed after Angela went back to work. She pulled out her computer and finished her article about Milledgeville, its history, its uses, and its cemeteries. Of course, she didn't mention Ross's mom. Some people would assume that's why she went, others wouldn't have a clue of the significance of such an article just before Christmas.

***

The Saturday before Christmas brought the hustle and bustle of shoppers to malls and shops. For the wedding party, it meant a trip to Atlanta, separately, to pick up the rest of the wedding party attire. Dorie and Angela headed for Lori's Bridals, and Ross and Riley drove to Atlanta Kilts.

Dorie and Angela left from Daelin. They drove to Lori's Bridals to pick up the veil that the seamstress was attaching the pearls to from the damaged Grandma MacAvoy veil. Then they needed to shop for shoes.

Lori, the proprietor, greeted them. "Dorie, I was excited for you to see the veil. It turned out fantastic."

She led Dorie and Angela to the alterations department and put Dorie in a dressing room. The seamstress brought the veil in and carefully attached it in Dorie's hair, arranging it around her, even though she was just wearing jeans and a turtleneck.

"C'est magnifique, Miss Dorie." The seamstress clapped her hands. You must go out and look in the mirror."

Dorie walked out to the multiple paned mirrors where Angela was waiting.

"Oh, Dorie! It's a work of art." Angela jumped to her feet to join Dorie at the mirror.

Dorie cried when she looked in the mirror. It fit perfectly around her face with the wide embroidered lace including the silver beading from the old veil. In the back, veil pooled on the ground where the embroidered and beaded lace completed its circumference around the veil. Within the soft netting, the tiny pearls had been expertly sewn, one at a time. As Dorie turned, the silver beads sparkled, and the tiny pearls caught the light with a soft glimmer.

"It's beautiful!" Dorie wept. It was as if the dreams she never knew she had for this wedding had come true with this finishing touch. "It was so worth doing. You did a spectacular job. Thank you!"

The seamstress bowed to her. "It was worth every stitch to see you in it, Miss Dorie."

Angela handed Dorie a tissue.

"I am so overwhelmed, Angie. This isn't like me to cry over pearls and lace. Tomboy, remember?" Dorie wiped her face and blew her nose. "I wouldn't have even bought this veil if it hadn't been for Grandma MacAvoy's veil."

"It's okay, Dorie. Even us tomboys are women inside." Angela helped her remove the heavy comb and hang the veil with utmost care in a garment bag. "All those hormones catch up to all of us."

"If the veil gets crumpled, steam it with a garment steamer or steam up the bathroom and let it hang in there." Lori hugged her. "Now about those shoes."

Dorie and Angela went to the shoe department and tried on shoes.

Lori brought Dorie a box. "When I saw you in your dress, and now in the veil, I thought these shoes would be perfect."

She opened the box to reveal a pair of pumps with ivory lace that came over the side of the foot. Crystals formed a flower on the side of the toe. They would match the gown and the veil exactly.

Angela went wild. "Those are spectacular! It doesn't matter how much they cost, you are getting those shoes!"

Dorie tried on the four-inch heels. She twirled and looked in the mirror. "They're perfect, except they're so tall."

"Not a problem, Dorie. They also come in a two- and three-quarter heel."

Dorie tried those on too. When faced with a four-inch or a three-inch heel, she thought of those stairs. She bought them in a three-inch heel. Even then, she planned to walk down the stairs barefoot, then slip them on at the bottom. Maybe Ross could do a Cinderella-thing and put them on her then.

Angela found a beautiful pair of glittering burgundy peep-toes with four-inch heels that matched her dress perfectly.

***

Meanwhile, across Atlanta at Atlanta Kilts, Ross tried on his Grandpa Ross's kilt. It looked brand-new after repair and cleaning.

"Dorie will not know what hit her when she sees you in that at the bottom of the stairs." Riley paraded in the rental version of the Ross kilt.

"The question is, 'Will she forgive me?'" Ross worked with the Ross brooch to get it in the right place. "It's not a tuxedo. She was quite specific about the tuxedo part."

"No, man, you couldn't wear that generic red

plaid at your wedding. You're a Scot, you have principles about plaid." Riley affected a poor Scottish accent. "How do I look?"

"Great. I think it's perfect. She loves me, she'll give me this, don't you think?"

The clerk adjusted the tartan and brooch for him. "It's fantastic, man. Be proud of your heritage. A wedding is the perfect time to celebrate it." Then the clerk presented the Ross sash and the Luckenbooth double heart brooch with the garnet gem for him to give Dorie. "Aye, and this is the best way to show her your undying love, welcoming her into your clan. And here's the handfasting ribbon made from the Ross tartan."

Ross grinned and shook his head. "Aye, it's a beauty."

"As is the bride." Riley clapped him on the back. "I love it when a plan comes together."

They undressed, carefully repackaged it all, and headed back to Helen.

Chapter 24

Christmas Eve Eve Eve happenings …

Dorie woke with a start in the middle of the night, really the early morning of December 22, what her family called Christmas Eve Eve Eve. She knew someone who had a key! Melody had been letting Star in and out the whole fall. If she had it hanging in the diner, any number of people could have access to it. But how did the person get in after the new locks were in? Ross had all the new keys but the two, deadbolt and knob, he had given her. Unless he had thought to take a pair to Melody without telling her.

Star moaned in her open crate.

"I know, baby, I woke you up, didn't I?"

Dorie turned on the light next to the bed in the Andrews's cottage. Star turned around in the crate and flopped onto the crate mat. Then she looked at Dorie accusingly before closing her eyes and going back to sleep.

"Great, now I'm awake alone." She got out of bed and looked out down the dark driveway. Some early birds were chirping. The ground looked frosty, appropriate for days before Christmas.

Then Dorie saw a shadow cross the driveway. She dressed in jeans, a heavy cowl-necked red sweater, and burgundy suede boots. She threw on her winter coat, left Star in her crate, then went outside to check it out.

It was cold, and every sound seemed amplified. The grass crunched beneath her boots. The clear sky allowed the stars to twinkle in the cold dark. Her breath was visible in clouds of mist. It seemed almost magical. If it had been Christmas Eve, Dorie would have checked the sky for a sleigh and reindeer. She crept around the house and looked for an intruder.

Nobody there.

The side window opened. Ethan stuck his head out. "What are you doing?"

"I thought I saw somebody." Dorie turned to see him. "But I don't see anyone now."

"It's three AM! Why are you up?"

Dorie shivered and stuck her hands in her coat pockets. "I had a realization that woke me up. Then I saw a shadow cross the driveway."

"Go back to bed." Ethan pulled his head in just as a blazing pain struck the back of Dorie's head. "Dorie!"

The next thing Dorie knew she was being loaded into an ambulance, and her head was pounding.

"Welcome back to us, Miss Dorie. How do you feel?" The EMT had hooked up an IV and was checking her blood pressure. "Bet you have a headache."

"Sure do. What happened?" Dorie winced as the ambulance doors slammed shut.

"You were hit on the back of the head with a baseball bat."

It hurt to think. "Who would do that?" Dorie let her head rest on the gurney pillow. "Did Ethan see anything?"

"He's talking to Captain McDonough now. Our job is to make sure you're okay. Just rest. We'll be at Daelin Medical Center in just a couple of minutes."

The next thing Dorie knew she was in the Emergency Department, and nurses were around her taking vitals and such.

"It's okay, Dorie. We're taking care of you. We'll stitch up the back of your head and do some diagnostics. Your fiancé is in the waiting room. Do you want him back here with you?"

She tried to nod, but it hurt too much. "Yes, send him to me."

***

Ross paced the waiting room in his regular jeans and plaid flannel shirt. Ethan Andrews was there in his sweats. Riley was there in uniform.

"You might as well sit down, Ross. We could be here for hours." Riley sipped coffee from the waiting room coffeemaker.

"Why would someone go out of their way to hit Dorie with a baseball bat? Her family is arriving this afternoon. Now they want to come here instead of the house in Helen. This is not what Dorie wants for our wedding."

Riley gave a puzzling look. "What if the wedding has been the focus all along? Who would not want you marrying Dorie?"

"Dorie went all the way to Milledgeville to

determine that your mom was not involved." Ethan poured coffee too. "Who else is left that could get into your house? Dorie said she was up because of a revelation about keys."

Ross stopped and looked at Ethan. "She's been asking me about who else has keys for weeks. I forgot to tell her there was a set at Melody's Diner. She thought of someone?"

"Apparently it woke her up. Then she saw a shadow on the driveway, dressed, and went outside to see who was there." Ethan shook his head. "I wish I'd seen more than the baseball bat headed for her head. Nobody was out there by the time I threw on sweats and called for EMTs."

"We have the bat, Ross." Riley stood and put a hand on his shoulder. "Maybe we can lift prints."

"I know, which are useless if the prints aren't already in the system. Maybe Dorie remembers her revelation." Ross sighed and slumped into a worn-out waiting room chair. "I'm getting so tired of Dorie being hurt because of her job or me."

Angela arrived in the waiting room with coffee for Ross, Riley, Ethan, and Dorie. "How's our girl? I just heard she was brought here by ambulance. What happened?"

A white-coated doctor with a computer tablet came from the Emergency Department. "Ross MacAvoy? Dorie Hudson would like you to come back and be with her."

Angela handed him the drink caddy and put his and Dorie's in it before he hurried down the hall to Dorie's room in the Emergency Department.

Ross pulled back the curtain and entered. "I

bring coffee from Angela."

"Fantastic." Dorie sat up in the bed wearing a hospital gown with her jeans. Blood seemed to be everywhere, down the gown and in the towel she held on the back of her head.

Ross leaned over and kissed her.

She winced. "Gently for now. Hopefully dramatically at the wedding in two days."

He handed her the coffee.

Dorie took the cup and sipped it. "Oh yes, I feel better all ready."

"Ethan tells me you had an 'Aha' moment about keys." Ross sat in a chair beside the bed. "Do you remember what it was?"

Just then, the doctor entered the room. "Good morning, Ross. Your girl here is back with us." He turned to Dorie. "So, the good news is you have an extremely hard head. Bet Ross already knew that." He laughed. "There is a slight fracture of the skull, but I think it will be fine. Come back if you are faint, nauseated, dizzy, headachy. I know, the wedding is in two days. The nurse told me. The big question is, 'Can you walk down the aisle?'"

"The stairs. Can I walk down the stairs at the Doll House?" Dorie winced. "Without pain?"

"The stairs are trickier, I'll grant you. We're going to glue your gash closed. We'll be careful to keep your hair as much out of it as possible. Be careful with a veil or tiara with a comb that might breach the wound." The doctor looked at the wound again. "It's pretty jagged, but I think you can avoid it. Be careful with hair washing."

"What about the honeymoon?" Ross felt like

scum asking, but he didn't want to take any chance of hurting her. "Flying for instance."

The doctor scratched his chin. "Honeymoon? Avoid swimming or hot tubs. Be cautious of climbing ladders. Give yourself a chance to heal. Hopefully, the marriage will last longer than the honeymoon." He winked. "Just take it easy. Rest for today."

He signed the chart electronically and hurried out.

"Ladders?" Dorie asked. "What kind of honeymoon did he have in mind?"

"Maybe a Robinson Crusoe tree house?" Ross waggled his eyebrows, hoping she would laugh.

Dorie giggled then covered her face. "No, don't make me laugh. It hurts too much."

A nurse brought in an icepack and asked her to lay down as best she could with the icepack on the back of her head.

Chapter 25

Dorie's family arriving ...

Ross walked out into the waiting room to update their friends. "The doctor finally concluded that Dorie should rest, and that she'd only do that in the hospital for the day."

"Uh, oh. The ED personnel know Dorie too well." Angela laughed. "This is a good thing, Ross."

"He plans to discharge Dorie around three this afternoon, in time for her family's arrival. I have final preparations for the Hudsons' arrival and dinner to prepare." Ross felt a little lost at trying to entertain her family by himself.

Riley clapped him on the back. "No problem. I'll collect her when she's discharged and drive her up the mountain road to see them and have dinner, if I can wangle an invitation."

Ross nodded. "Of course."

"Then I can bring her back to Ethan's tonight." Riley hugged his shoulders. "It will be okay, friend."

"They're in the process of moving her to a room now. I said my good-byes. The Hudsons are already on the road." Ross felt the prickly sensation of panic starting in his chest. "I'm not sure I can do this."

"Don't worry, Ross. I'll sit with her. I got my replacement for Christmas Eve and tomorrow night to go ahead and work today too." Angela hugged him tight. "We've got lots of things we can talk about before the wedding."

"Dorie has already filed her article for the paper. She's clear until you get back from your mysterious honeymoon." Ethan shook his hand.

"Thanks, guys, you're the best friends we could have." Ross's voice caught in his throat. He'd best leave before he cried in front of them. "See ya later, then.

***

Dorie woke to Angela sitting at her side.

"Ross?" Dorie felt so groggy. She grabbed the back of her head and felt the glue holding her scalp together. "I'd run too."

"That's ridiculous. Ross is in Helen getting the house ready for your family." Angela patted her hand. "And he's even cooking dinner for them."

"I was supposed to do that." Dorie felt the tears forming. "This whole thing is a disaster. Can't we even get married like a normal couple? I'm feeling star-crossed."

Angela climbed into the bed next to her. "Dorie. You love Ross, and Ross loves you. There's nothing star-crossed about that. He loves you. Does anything else really matter?"

"I suppose not. Still I ought to be there when my family gets there." Tears leaked down her cheeks.

"Hey, you're only here until about three. Then they'll discharge you, and Riley is going to drive you to Helen." Angela wiped Dorie's tears with a corner of the hospital-issue blanket. "Riley is going to bring you back to Ethan's after dinner."

Dorie sniffed. "Rehearsal tomorrow?"

"Yes, ma'am. It's all going to be fine, promise."

"Thank you for keeping me sane, Angie." Dorie wrapped an arm around her.

"Hey, that's what the matron of honor is supposed to do, right?"

A nurse entered the room. "But she's not supposed to be in the hospital bed with the bride."

Angela jumped out of the bed and into a chair by the bed.

Dorie giggled, and soon Angela was giggling uncontrollably.

"So, Miss Dorie, you're getting married on Christmas Eve?" The nurse checked her vitals from the machine she was hooked to. "Dr. Sinclair has already signed your discharge orders, but you are not to leave before three o'clock. I suggest you rest. I'll be checking on you. Don't be afraid to sleep."

"I have my book from the car." Angela waved it in the air. "I'll read, she'll sleep."

Dorie tried to nod, but she thought better of it. "I'll try. There's just so much to think about."

"Like your handsome groom, Mr. Ross MacAvoy. He is a sight for tired eyes, I'll give you that." The nurse fanned herself with a file as she left the room. "Save some strength for the honeymoon, Miss Dorie."

***

Ross arrived in Helen and let himself in the house. Even Star was down at the Andrews'. The house seemed to echo.

The first thing he did was drag the Christmas tree from the attic and set it up. Dorie had said they didn't need a tree at the house, no one would be there to appreciate it. But … it was Christmas. They'd open packages with her family tomorrow night after the rehearsal and dinner. It would be odd to sit in the living room opening presents without a proper tree.

Once he got the tree up, Ross wrapped the presents they had for Dorie's brothers and mom and dad. Then he wrapped the gifts for Riley and Angela, especially as they were their witnesses. Gifts for Melody and Jenny also went under the tree. When it was done, Ross plugged in the lights and stepped back to assess his work. It looked like Christmas. That's all he could ask.

It felt odd doing all this without Dorie.

After a bite of lunch, Ross tackled the kitchen. The plan was chuck roast like the Hudsons had enjoyed on Sundays after church. Chuck roast, potatoes, carrots, onions – all in the roaster for several hours. Then came strawberry pretzel salad. All that was left was to heat the green beans and rolls.

Ross extended the new kitchen table and set it for eight – five Hudsons from St. Louis, Riley, Dorie, and himself. Once everything was ready to go, Ross went out on the front porch and hung a wreath on the front door to welcome Dorie. He had so much more decorating that he would have done, but there was no time left to do more.

Riley's SUV pulled into the front drive. Ross ran to get Dorie because she probably shouldn't run to him.

"Ah, darling, I've been so worried about you."

He picked her up as soon as she stepped from the vehicle.

"I missed you too, but I think I can walk." Dorie threw her arms around his neck.

"Don't ever let go." Ross held her close.

"Don't plan to, sweetheart." She kissed him.

Ross carried her to the porch. Honking began as he set her down.

"They're here!" Dorie held onto him. "It's happening."

"It is." Ross wrapped an arm around her, wishing he could never let go.

The Hudsons' Excursion pulled into the drive. Her brothers were out of the car before her dad shifted into park.

"The three Musketeers. I've heard of you." The first brother to the porch was Terrence. Everyone called him Terry, and he was the oldest. His hair was dark brown as were his eyes. He was at least six-foot-four-inches tall. When he reached Dorie, he grabbed her up in his arms. "Ross, good to see you again. This must be Riley." He set Dorie down and shook hands with the men. "Ooh, something smells good."

Meanwhile, the others were emptying the car of luggage, wrapped gifts, and garment bags. Riley strode across the yard to help with the luggage. Dorie hurried to her mom, and they embraced. Ross followed Dorie to the car, took some of the wrapped packages from the back, then carried them into the house.

Aaron, a tall lanky confectioner's sugar blonde second brother, brought in luggage. "Where do you want these bags, Ross?" Aaron was a seminary student.

"Just put them at the bottom of the stairs, Aaron." Ross went back to the door and took packages from Dorie who followed him to the tree.

Ross pulled Dorie into his lap and sat on the floor facing the tree.

"I thought we weren't decorating for Christmas." She wrapped her arms around his neck.

"I changed my mind." Ross nuzzled her neck.

Terry joined them. "You guys stay there. What can I do?"

"Pull the roast out of the oven." Ross hugged Dorie. "Is it wrong to let the company serve dinner?"

"Hey, we're not company, we're family." Alex was brother number three, and he was six foot five inches. He worked as an architect. "We'll serve dinner."

Chapter 26

Attic visitor revealed …

Once dinner was complete and the kitchen cleaned up, everyone was tired. Riley and Dorie decided it was time to head back to Daelin.

Ross hugged her and kissed her then stood on the porch to watch them leave. He waved then stayed staring at the road.

"Hey, lover boy, it's cold out here." Terry had joined him on the porch. "Come in and help us figure out our sleeping arrangements."

Ross put Dorie's parents in the Rose Bedroom, since it was more feminine. Then he took a plastic drinking straw and cut into three unequal lengths. He put them in his fist, so they were sticking out evenly.

"Okay, guys, I've got three sections of straw. Long straw gets the proper bedroom, medium straw gets the pull-out sofa in Dorie's office, short straw gets the new sofa or old futon."

The brothers groaned, moaned, and whined.

"Well, there's always the chaise lounge chairs on the deck." Ross extended his fist.

Aaron stepped up. "I'll pull first."

"Nope, firstborn goes first." Terry shoved Aaron away and pulled a straw. "It seems pretty long."

Aaron pulled slowly to extend the suspense. "Longer than yours, big bro! Do you know how rare it is for the middle brother to get the best choice?"

"Okay, Alex, your turn." Ross extended his fist to him.

"Short straw. Youngest one with third best. It figures." Alex flopped on the couch. "New couch, Ross. That's my choice."

Ross helped the guys get settled. He headed up into the attic from the second floor to get a sleeping bag for Alex to use. His arms were full when he came back down. He didn't slide the bolt back on the door.

He made sure everybody had a plastic cup in the bathrooms, clean towels, and enough blankets. Then he turned off the tree, made a pass through the kitchen and started the dishwasher, then made sure the front, garage, and deck doors were double-locked.

"Tomorrow, I want to see your renovations and check out your double flight attic stairs and attic. We have basements for our junk in the Midwest." Alex flipped off the lamp at the end of the couch. "Good night, Ross. Try to get to sleep. We'll be fine."

It was late when Ross finally finished brushing his teeth and climbed into bed. He was glad he'd added the private master bath over the garage. He flipped off the light and fell asleep.

Not long after, the light came on in the hallway. Toilet run. He rolled over to go back to sleep. A flash of silver caught his eye. A knife on its downward path to his chest.

The attacker shrieked. Ross yelled out. He rolled away from the knife onto the floor.

Voices called out, and the light in the bedroom came on. Terry grabbed the attacker. Dorie's dad rushed to the side of the bed to check on Ross. Soon everyone in the house was in the master bedroom.

Dorie's dad helped Ross up.

Dorie's mom was in the doorway crying and had her hand over her mouth. Alex and Aaron were crowded into the space.

Ross finally saw his attacker. "Why are you trying to kill me? Emmie? What are you doing?"

"I would never try to kill you, Ross. I thought Dorie would be sleeping here with her family tonight."

Dorie's dad cried out. "Why are you trying to kill my daughter?"

Emmie turned to him with a scary vengeance Ross had never seen before in her. "Because she is taking my Ross away from me. He is supposed to marry me."

Ross called 911.

The Helen police arrived, cuffed Emmie, and took her to Helen lockup.

Ross sat stunned on the couch next to Alex after they'd left. Everyone else went back to bed.

"Hey, my bed. Remember, I drew a straw for this couch."

Ross stood. Alex pulled his legs back up into the vacated seat.

"You know the funny part of this whole thing?" Ross tried to calm his breathing. "The motion sensor light I installed in the hall saved my life tonight."

"You have an odd sense of humor, brother."

"I need to get to Daelin." Ross needed to be with Dorie. Not tomorrow morning, now. He got his coat from the hall tree, wrapped his scarf around the collar, and headed out the door.

Ross started Grandpa's truck and revved it a couple times to warm the engine. Then he called Dorie, put it in gear, and turned out on the mountain road to Daelin.

"Hello?" She sounded groggy.

"I'm headed to Daelin. We need to talk. Our attic visitor revealed herself tonight."

"What happened?" She sounded awake now.

"I'll tell you when I get there. Turn off your phone. I don't want you to hear this from anyone else. I should be there between 30-40 minutes. It's late, probably not much traffic."

"I'm turning it back on if you're not here by then in case you're on the side of the road in your grandpa's truck. Drive safely."

"Go to the cottage to wait for me. Get the K-cup machine ready to make some coffee."

"Didn't I get fussed at for being out in the middle of the night yesterday?"

"I know. It's safe now." Ross felt a sense of relief to say those words to Dorie.

"I love you, Ross."

"Love you too, Dorie."

After Ross hung up, he called Riley.

"Hello, Ross." Riley sounded like he'd been awake already.

"I was nearly killed tonight by our attic visitor."

"Who was it? Was it who I thought it was?"

"If you thought it was Emmie, you were right."

"You knew it was her, didn't you?" Riley didn't seem at all surprised. "When did you know for sure?"

"The missing keys at Melody's. Then the artist rendering pretty much cinched it. I'm headed to Dorie."

"Do you need to sleep on my couch tonight?"

"Yeah, but I don't know when it will be."

"Key is under the mat, bro."

Chapter 27

Christmas Eve Eve activities …

Dorie jumped out of bed and pulled on her jeans, turtleneck, boots, and coat. She touched the ivory gown hanging in the bedroom. It was Christmas Eve Eve, the day before Christmas Eve. Today was the rehearsal at the Doll House. She really hoped her dad would hold on tight while she walked down those stairs. What was she thinking? The shoes and veil also waited. It all looked perfect. With the visitor out of the way, maybe it could be.

Then Dorie slipped out the back door and unlocked the cottage at the end of the driveway. She turned up the heat. Then she filled the reservoir of the K-cup machine and fixed his and her coffee cups with their favorite add-ins. She watched the clock, anticipating his arrival. She turned on her phone, afraid he was stuck somewhere on that mountain road.

Dorie began to dial his number, but she heard the tap on the door. She jumped up to open it.

Ross grabbed her and held her so tight she thought she'd squeak. "I love you so much."

"I love you still." They kissed building to a crescendo of love and passion. She didn't want to break it off, but she didn't want to wait this long and spoil their wedding night. And she wanted to know what had happened. Dorie stopped the kiss before it went farther than they really wanted it to go. "Two days. Just two days to wait now." She extricated herself from his grasp.

"You're right." Ross looked downcast but nodded agreement.

Dorie started the coffee once he let her go while Ross took off his coat, scarf, and gloves. "How are you feeling, darling?"

"Still have a headache, but it's better." She handed him a cup with coffee.

"Good. I hate that you're not going to feel well for our big day."

"I don't plan to let it bother me. I'll have more important things to think about." Dorie finished making her cup of coffee and sat down on the loveseat with him. "So, tell me what happened."

"Emmie tried to kill me. The motion sensor saved my life."

"Why would Emmie try to kill you?" Dorie set down her cup and threw her arms around him.

"She thought you'd be in the bed since your family was there." Ross held her as close as he dared.

"I thought she liked me. Why?"

"She said I was supposed to marry her."

Dorie was silent for a moment, trying to think with her aching head. "The baseball bat, too?"

"Probably. She's in Helen PD lockup right now. Riley will probably charge her as well."

They sat together for a long while, sometimes talking, mostly just being together. Finally, Ross stood.

"I need to get some sleep. I'll be at Riley's."

Dorie jumped up and kissed him good-bye. "Merry Christmas Eve Eve."

Ross laughed. "To you, too, my love."

***

Ross drove over to Riley's townhouse. He found the key under the mat and let himself in. As he stepped in the door, the light flipped on.

"Hey, it's late. I fell asleep waiting for you. You haven't been doing anything inappropriate, have you?"

Ross pulled off his coat. "Nope. Merry Christmas Eve Eve."

"But my name's not Eve." Riley stood and stretched. "You need some sleep."

"After that joke, I think you do too."

Riley helped Ross put the folded comforter on the couch for Ross's bedding. "Can we talk for a second? I know you worry about Dorie's safety. I think you should let Dorie take the Daelin PD job."

Ross shook his head. "Why? She's a good reporter."

"True, but she's a better detective." Riley put his hand on his shoulder. "I need her working for Daelin PD. I can keep an eye on her, especially come spring when you're watching over the Chattahoochee Forest."

Ross hesitated.

"Don't worry. There's no need to be jealous."

"But you're Chief of Police. I'm nobody. My

business failed. I'm unemployed. My mother was an insane murderer. You could offer her so much more."

"She loves you. I know she's yours. I would never, never, compromise her. You have my word."

"You could be right. I'll tell her it's okay, but it's up to her to decide." Ross flopped onto the couch. "Let's sleep."

Riley padded off to bed while Ross opened the folded comforter and snuggled in its folds. He knew he wouldn't be sleeping, but at least he could pretend to rest.

When the clock dinged at six, Ross heard Riley in the shower. He got off the couch and folded up the comforter and started the coffeepot.

When the shower stopped, Ross waited outside the bathroom for Riley to relinquish it.

"Whoa! You surprised me, Ross." Riley nearly dropped his towel.

"Sorry. I wanted to get an early start. Got a few things to do today." Ross dashed into the bathroom fog and started it up again.

"Did you sleep at all?" Riley called to him.

"Not really." Ross closed the bathroom door.

A heat and serve breakfast sandwich and another cup of coffee later, Ross was on his way to pick up Dorie to help him buy a new truck. He'd learned his lesson on the SUV deal: Always include the wife in the buying a vehicle business.

She was standing on the driveway waiting on him.

Dorie climbed in the old truck then leaned over

for a kiss.

Ross kissed her again, 'cause why not? "One more day."

"It can't get here soon enough. Meanwhile let's get you truck that can get you in and out of the Chattahoochee Forest come spring."

By lunch, the bargaining was over, and Dorie drove the new truck up the mountain behind Ross and Grandpa MacAvoy's truck. At least if the old girl croaked on the side of the road, Dorie would be there to give him a lift.

They arrived at the house to mayhem. The three brothers were tossing a football in the backyard. Dorie's mom was wrapping more gifts, as though there weren't enough already around the tree, down the wall, and onto the kitchen table. Dorie's dad was grilling burgers on the grill on the patio outside the garage door.

Dorie picked up Alex's sleeping bag, rolled it up and stuffed it behind the couch. Ross emptied the dishwasher and got out the appropriate dishware for lunch. Chips and burger condiments joined the wrapping paper on the table.

"Burgers are ready. Good for you guys to come. Where ya been?" Dorie's dad brought in a tray of charred burgers. "Just the way you like them, Dorie. Black on the outside."

Ross gave her a quizzical look, and Dorie began to laugh. Then she grabbed the back of her head and ran for the bathroom. Ross followed her and held her hair as she vomited. He got her a cold, damp washcloth to wipe her face and put on the back of her head. He helped her up the stairs and put her in the slit sheets of their bed. Then he left her after turning out the lights.

"Everything okay?" Dorie's mom met Ross at the bottom of the stairs.

"We've done a lot this morning. Her head hurts. We'll save her a burger for later."

Dorie's dad called the brothers in from the yard for lunch.

***

When Dorie woke, it was two PM, but she felt better. There was much to do, though.

"There you are." A chorus of men's voices greeted her from the table where they were playing Yahtzee.

Ross jumped up from the table and jogged to her. "Do you feel better? Should you call the doctor? Are you okay?"

Dorie kissed him to shut him up. "I'm okay. I just overdid it this morning."

"We saved you lunch. Don't say you're not hungry. You need to eat."

"Okay, relax." She allowed him to guide her to the kitchen and poured her a Coke while he nuked her burger.

After she ate, they opened wedding gifts from Missouri.

At four, they gathered at the Doll House to rehearse, in Ross's words, falling down the stairs.

The rehearsal dinner was at Melody's Diner, without Emmie.

Chapter 28

Then it was finally Christmas Eve…

The day was a whirlwind of activities. It was finally the day of the wedding, but it was also Christmas Eve.

The conspiracy began early to keep Dorie and Ross apart.

"Bad luck to see the bride before the wedding." Angela declared to Dorie as they loaded the gown, shoes, veil, and suitcase into the SUV. "I'll be taking this to the Doll House while you rest today. There's already been enough excitement this week. I'll meet Marjorie and help her with the flowers while I'm there."

"I'm supposed to just sit here and wait for this afternoon?"

"You got it, girlie. Gotta run." Angela turned out of the Andrews' driveway with Dorie's gown, shoes, veil, and suitcase.

***

"Don't worry, you'll see her forever after

tonight." Riley goaded him as they pulled into the parking lot of the Doll House B&B. "Besides there's a lot to do before four o'clock."

"What? We've got the kilts and accoutrements. I've packed for the honeymoon."

"I can't believe you're taking her to Scotland. I've always wanted to go. And staying for Hogmanay. I'm jealous, bro." Riley jumped out of Ross's truck and grabbed the garment bags from behind the seat.

Ross got out and grabbed his suitcase from the back.

The scene inside the Doll House was literally mayhem. Marjorie was draping greenery everywhere it could be hooked. Poinsettias sat on every square inch of floor and on each step. People were running to and fro with platters of food. The bakers were arranging the tiered bridal cake in the center of the antique dining table. Folding chairs fitted with white covers sat in rows facing the fireplace. Two stockings were hung with care there labeled Ross and Dorie.

"You're dressing in Room 2, down here behind the staircase. Dorie is dressing in your room for the night upstairs, Room 4." Angela waved her arms in the appropriate directions. She seemed quite frantic to Ross.

"Angela, I think you've had too much coffee." Ross had to yell over the vacuum cleaner. "Relax. It will all be fine. Where's Dorie?"

"Dorie's at the Andrews' house. I'll go pick her up around two-thirty. And I haven't had any coffee yet, but there's an urn in the kitchen if you want some." She ran off to the back of the house.

Ross set his suitcase down behind the folding chairs and found Marjorie. "Do you think it's a good idea to put those poinsettias on the steps? Dorie's coming down those steps in a wedding dress with her dad. She's not very graceful. I'd hate to see them being knocked off."

Marjorie nodded. "Maybe every other step then."

Ross smacked himself in the forehead. "Seriously?" But Marjorie had flown away to respace the poinsettias.

Riley rushed in and grabbed Ross's suitcase. "You gotta come see this room."

Ross followed Riley, dodging the vacuum, the florist, the bakers, Angela, and the ladder with greenery left to be hung.

"This is crazy." Ross tripped over the vacuum cord, pulling it from the outlet. "Sorry. I'm plugging it back in."

He finally stumbled into Room 2. "Wow. This is nice."

Riley had taken kilts and such from the garment bags and hung them on hooks on the wall. "Need anything from the suitcase for the ceremony?"

"I don't think so." Ross felt his head spinning. Maybe it was a good thing Dorie wasn't here. Her head was already dizzy from the baseball bat incident. He still couldn't believe Emmie could do such a thing.

"Hey! Earth to Ross!" Riley was snapping his fingers in front of Ross's face. "What are you thinking?"

"Actually, I was thinking about Emmie. I still can't believe it was her."

"I know what you mean. Psycho was not a term I'd have used in connection with her."

"Do you think my mom was somehow to blame?" Ross couldn't believe the repercussions a birthday party could spread.

Riley shoved Ross down on the bed. "Mental illness is not a virus. We were there too. We're not trying to bludgeon or stab anyone. Try to let it go, bro. We all cope with trauma in our own way. I'm going for coffee. Want any?"

"Why not? It's going to be a long day." Ross laid back on the bed. "On second thought, maybe I'll try to sleep for an hour."

***

Riley headed to the kitchen for that coffee. A young woman with light brown hair tied up in a ponytail had her back to him.

"Excuse me, can I get a cup of coffee." Riley tapped the woman on the shoulder.

"Black, no cream, no sugar, right Chief McDonough?" She turned around and smiled. "You haven't called me yet."

"Jenny? When Ross said Melody and Jenny from the B&B were handling food, I never thought it was you." He'd nearly said, 'my Jenny,' but that would be premature and presumptuous.

"I work the breakfast shift here then go into town to the café." She shrugged. "A girl's got to make a living, after all."

"So, you'll be here for the wedding this afternoon?" Riley sure hoped so.

"Yes, I'm taking off from the café to work the wedding. It pays better." She handed him a cup of coffee. "I gather you are the best man."

"Of course, I'm the best man." He wanted to add 'for you.' Guess it was something about weddings that made him sentimental.

"There's a buzz around the house that you and Ross are wearing kilts this evening." She smiled. "Now that's something I'd like to see."

"Aye, it will be grand." Riley's Scottish accent needed work. "I never wore a kilt until Ross took me to Atlanta Kilts. I may need to purchase a McDonough kilt someday."

"Will you wear one for your wedding?" She leaned against the counter and crossed her arms.

"Depends on the bride, I suspect. Ross is taking a risk with not telling Dorie about it. I guess he knows her well enough to know it won't matter to her what he wears." Riley sipped his coffee keeping an eye on Jenny. "What would you prefer?"

"I guess I'll have to see you look in one this afternoon, won't I?" Jenny stood straight and leaned toward him and gave him a kiss on the cheek. "Gotta go. Lots to do."

Riley's heart seemed to be out of sync after that kiss.

***

Dorie was restless. She'd played with Star and made Christmas cookies with Lilah.

She wrote an article about Emmie, Ross, Riley, Jared, and the ill-fated birthday party. She included the info about Sally. She also told the story of Jeanine Ross MacAvoy and her death at Milledgeville

Central State Hospital. Dorie added the information about Emmie and the attic visitations, including the night Emmie tried to kill Ross. Ethan said it would be in the New Year's paper as the end of the story.

Dorie showered then painted her fingernails. Then she painted her toenails too.

After lunch, she called Ross.

"Hello, Dorie." He sounded chipper

"Hello, Ross. I am so bored here by myself." Dorie laid on the bed with her phone. "All I want is to be with you."

"Same here. Only a few more hours, and then you can never get rid of me." His laugh made her smile.

"Until you start your job with the National Forest Service, anyway."

"Speaking of jobs, Riley and I talked about the job he offered you with Daelin PD. If it's what you want to do, I won't stand in your way. It's your decision, not mine." He paused. "Dorie? What are you thinking?"

"I'm thinking that my husband is the head of my family who loves me the way Christ loves the church and gave himself for her. I know, without a shadow of a doubt, that you want wants good for me as well as good for us. I love you, Ross MacAvoy."

"Ah darling. I love you, too." A ruckus began in the background.

"What's that?" The sound was familiar. "My brothers. Guess my family just arrived."

"When will you be here?"

"Angela is picking me up about 2:00. I should be there just after 2:30."

"Meet me at the bottom of the stairs about 4:00?"

Dorie sighed. He really knew how to melt her heart. "That's the plan, sweetheart."

"Until then?"

"Until then, my love." Dorie hung up, satisfied, but still alone.

Chapter 29

A time to love and marry …

W hen Angela pulled into the driveway at 2:15, Dorie was coming apart at the seams.

"Where have you been? I've been standing here in the cold for fifteen minutes, afraid you wouldn't come for some reason, and I'd miss my wedding."

"Chill out, Dorie. All is well. You have plenty of time." Angela stayed in the driver's seat. "As worked up as you are, I'm going to drive your car up the mountain road."

Dorie huffed as she went around to the passenger's side. "Good thing you guys don't order me around all the other days of the year." She slammed the door once she was in.

"Relax, girlfriend. Everything is okay. The B&B looks beautiful. Jenny and Melody have been cooking and fixing all day. Marjorie's flowers and decorating is everything you could imagine."

"Really?" Dorie felt small and unnecessary. "Nobody needed me at all?"

"Well, of course, everyone needs you. Let us do this for you and Ross. You're only getting married once." Angela turned onto the mountain road. "You'll be there soon."

Dorie stepped into a Christmas wonderland when she entered the Doll House. Everything was perfect. She smelled cookies and turkey and dressing. The smell of cider wafted through the house with orange and nutmeg overtones. Christmas carols played over the house sound system. A fire roared in the fireplace behind the pastor's podium.

When she gasped, everyone turned around and clapped. Riley and Ross were missing, though.

"Where are Riley and Ross?"

"Room 2, sequestered from seeing the bride." Terry gave her a big hug. "You look beautiful. Why not get married in jeans?"

"No. For once, I am going to be dressed appropriately." Dorie pushed him away. The rest of her family exclaimed over her.

She went into the kitchen to see and smell all the goodies being prepared. "Thank you, ladies. It all smells like an old-fashioned Christmas. That was my hope."

"Everything's going great. We'll be able to eat as soon as the ceremony is done. Take a look at the cake. Heather at the bakery outdid herself." Melody offered her a freshly baked cookie, which Dorie devoured.

Dorie went into the dining room and oohed and aahed over the cake. Then she slipped into the back hallway and rapped at Room 2.

"Come in." Riley's voice came from behind the door.

"I don't think that's what you want me to do." Dorie stood as close to the door as she could. "Ross, are you there?"

From just the other side of the door, Ross spoke up. "I'm here, Dorie. I'm so glad you're finally here."

"The house looks fantastic." Dorie leaned her forehead on the door. "I guess I'll be going upstairs and getting ready."

"I'll see you at four, darling."

"I'll be there, sweetheart."

Alex appeared in the hallway. "What are you doing? You're not supposed to be back here. Come on, I'll help you up the stairs."

The door to Room 4 was at the top of the stairs. Dorie opened it and saw her dress, veil, and shoes displayed together on an old wardrobe. She hurried in followed by her mom and Angela.

"Oh, Dorie. What a beautiful dress." Her mom examined it in detail. "You and Angela did a great job. Wish I could have been there too."

"Oh, no!" Dorie opened the suitcase on the bed frantically. "The pearls. I forgot the pearls."

"Nope." Angela handed the box to her from the dressing table. "They were in the garment bag with the dress."

Dorie dropped onto the bed. "I guess I'm more nervous than I thought."

"There's only an hour until showtime. You'd best start getting ready." Her mom pulled a camera from her purse. "I thought we could take some pictures with us girls."

Dorie hugged her mom. "That's a great idea."

Angela took the camera and took pictures of Dorie and her mom, the dress on the wardrobe, and the open box of pearls. Angela's burgundy dress hung on the closet door with glittery burgundy high heels underneath. She took a picture of that too.

At four o'clock, the Christmas music stopped, replaced by Beethoven's "Ode to Joy." Angela descended the stairs on Riley's arm.

The door to the bridal suite opened, and Dorie's dad met Dorie at the top of the stairs. Her mother was already seated with her brothers in the front row.

"My shoes?" Dorie grabbed her dad's arm.

"At the bottom of the stairs, as requested, milady." He hugged her. "You look beautiful, Dorie. Ross is a lucky man."

"No, Dad. I'm the lucky one." She kissed him. "I love you, Daddy."

"Shall we?"

At her nod, they began the descent to the bottom of the stairs. One of the poinsettias rocked on the edge of the stair, causing a gasp on Dorie's part. It decided to stay put.

As she cleared the staircase, Dorie saw Ross at the bottom, in full Bonnie Prince Charlie regalia in what could only be the Ross tartan. She smiled. It was even better than a tuxedo could have been.

Dorie reached the bottom of the staircase. Ross kneeled on one knee and slipped her shoes onto her feet. Then he took her arm from her dad and led her the rest of the way to the front of the room.

"You're beautiful," he whispered.

"So are you," she whispered back.

The ceremony was traditional except for the vows, the inclusion of the Christmas story, and the handfasting ritual.

"It was on a night like tonight that God was born as a baby boy. And on that night, angels sang, and shepherds searched for the baby. A star shone in the sky over Bethlehem like none had ever been, leading wise men to his home. It is this Christ that we worship at Christmas. The same Christ who in a Passover week thirty-three years later would give His life for us all. As you begin a Christian marriage, remember that Christ is the head of your home. It is to His standard alone you must live. Love one another, submit to one another. Ross, love Dorie in the way Christ loves the church and gave himself for it. Under sacrificial love, Dorie, love Ross and care for him in godly love. Be true to one another in righteous love."

The pastor paused. "You have written vows to one another. Ross, you may begin."

Ross turned to her with his heart in his eyes. Dorie gasped.

"Dorie, the Sunday you threw coffee on my shirt and tie was the day I knew that this day would happen. I fell in love with you that very moment. It was as though an angel had come with the sun sparkling in her hair. Grandfather MacAvoy told me that when you meet the woman you would love forever, you will know it. He was right. I love you just as I know I will love you for the rest of my life. You are my only true love. I pledge my life to you. That is my vow." Ross slipped the wedding ring onto her bare left ring finger and then slid the diamond on top of it.

Angela handed Dorie a tissue. Dorie dabbed at her eyes, unwilling to spoil her makeup.

"Ross, you are my hero, my friend, and my love. I will hold you close and love you only and always. I vow to uphold you and our home in the sight of God. You are my only true love. I pledge my life to you. That is my vow." Dorie slid a plain gold band onto his left ring finger.

Riley handed the tartan sash and brooch to Ross.

"You are now a member of clan Ross. This tartan sash indicates your permanent place in that clan. None can dare take you away from me." Ross looped the sash over one of her shoulders to the opposite hip. He fastened the garnet double heart brooch to the sash at her

hip.

Riley handed the handfasting ribbon to the pastor. He wrapped it around Dorie and Ross's clasped hands.

"The ancient Celts used handfasting as a sign of 'tying the knot'. The knot was meant to signify permanence of the vow. It was a sacred ceremony as permanent as any vows taken in the church. We honor this ritual before God." The pastor turned them around and held their bound hands for all to see. "By the authority invested in me by the state of Georgia and in the sight of Almighty God, I now declare you, husband and wife. You may kiss your bride, Ross."

And he did.

Epilogue

The honeymoon in Scotland …

The plane's wheels screeched as it landed at Edinburgh. After nine hours scrunched in a transatlantic flight, Dorie was overjoyed to get this part of the honeymoon over.

Ross grabbed her hand while they taxied to the terminal. "Scotland! Dorie, we're in Scotland."

Dorie had insisted on wearing her tartan sash on the plane. "And I'm dressed for it."

"I have planned so much for this trip. The Highlands, Loch Ness, Hadrian's Wall, Hogmanay, the Rosslyn Chapel. I also found the cutest boutique hotel, Grassmarket Hotel, just down the hill from Edinburgh Castle."

Dorie smiled at his excitement. "Aye, and we'll be together."

Ross kissed her. "Aye, we shall."

After passing through luggage retrieval, Customs, and Border Control, they hailed a cab in the cold, windy sunny day. Neither of them could sleep on the plane, but now weariness was setting in.

"Grassmarket Hotel." Ross told the driver who nodded and placed their luggage in thc 'boot.' He helped Dorie into the cab and climbed in after her.

They both watched the scenery fly by. It was Boxing Day, a National Bank Holiday, so the streets were nearly empty of their normally bustling traffic. The cab pulled up in front of the corner of Victoria and Grassmarket. A long, colorful curving street rose up the hill to the Royal Mile. Ross tipped the driver and grabbed their bags.

They hurried into the lobby of the Grassmarket Hotel. It was tiny. A large magnetic map of Edinburgh covered one wall. A long table with puzzles and games stood in front of it. The main desk was wedged into an alcove.

"G'morning. Happy Christmas." The young man appeared from the hallway to the pub. "We're servin' breakfast in the pub if you'd like to eat after checkin' in."

Dorie was starved. "Please! Is it part of the package?"

"Aye, it definitely can be, ma'am." He checked the computer. "Ye must be Ross and Dorie MacAvoy. You're the only ones checkin' in t'day. And staying through Hogmanay. Excellent."

"That's right." Ross wrapped his arm around Dorie as though she might fly away if he didn't. "It's our honeymoon." The look on his face included a silly grin of excitement and fulfillment all in one.

"I see here that you have a lovely room with a view on the lift side of the hotel." Dorie's look of incredulity caused the clerk to explain. "The hotel is a combination of previously existing establishments. One side has a lift, the other has stairs."

"Ah, I see." Dorie relaxed into Ross's embrace.

They were alone in a country where no one knew them in an ancient city perched on a giant volcanic rock. In Scotland, no less!

"Here's your key. Let us put your bags in your room. You go and have a Scottish breakfast." He handed Ross the key, came out of the alcove and pointed to the doors at the end of the hallway. The clerk pushed the 'lift' button and trundled the bags into it. "Enjoy your breakfast, tuck in. Then you may want to rest before hitting the town. It is a holiday."

The door slid closed on the clerk and the luggage. Ross shrugged and pointed the way to the pub at the end of the hall.

Steel cut oatmeal, breads of various kinds, eggs and ham, fruit, and something odd that turned out to be haggis were set up for self-service.

"Pick a spot. I'be right there with the coffee." A young waitress waved her arm around indicating pretty much the entire pub.

Dorie picked a dark corner. Ross slid the solid wood chair out for her, then he sat down next to her. The waitress arrived with the coffee. Sugar and milk were on the table for them.

"You can have any of what's out or I can place a special order. If'n you want to eat soon, I'd eat what's already provided. The cook was a bit too merry yesterday."

Dorie stifled a laugh. Ross laughed at her.

"Don't worry. We been havin' a laugh at his expense all mornin'." She placed the pot on the table for them and ran off to welcome another Boxing Day guest.

"Ah darling, no man could be happier than I."

Ross held her hand as though he'd never let go.

"We've got the rest of time to be happy together." Dorie sighed. "I think I'd best drink some coffee, so I can make it up in the 'lift' to our room before I drop from exhaustion."

He let go of her hand, so they could fix their coffee cups. "I'm going to scout out the buffet." He scraped the chair on the tiled floor. "I'll be back." He wangled those eyebrows that sent Dorie into peals of exhausted laughter.

When he returned, his plate looked like he'd sampled some of everything.

"Are you really going to eat all of that?" Dorie stood.

"Yes. Then I'm going to sleep beside you for the rest of the day and maybe most of the night. Tomorrow we must be up early for our tour of the Highlands."

Dorie nodded. "Very well. So, it begins."

The morning of the 27th, they were up before the sun in a region where the sun shines for fewer than seven hours a day in the winter. It was cold, and the wind blew icy flurries about their heads. They walked the curved Victoria Street up to the Royal Mile where they caught the tour bus. The sun rose around 8:30, one hour after the trip began. At about 9:30, the bus stopped for a break in the town of Pitlochry, a gateway to the Highlands. A hot coffee and then Ross and Dorie were on the bus again with their new friends for the day.

The tour bus took them through Cairngorms National Park, past Aviemore, through Inverness to

Loch Ness. At this point, Dorie and Ross had the choice of cruising Loch Ness, and looking for Nessie, or visiting a cultural center. No contest there, searching for Nessie was absolutely a requirement of this trip. The boat headed out into the loch. The breeze was so cold, most people took shelter in the cabin with their noses pressed against the glass in hopes of seeing the Loch Ness Monster.

"I don't know if we'll see Nessie, but the view inside the boat is nearly as entertaining." Dorie laughed behind her hand. "What do you think?"

"I think I love you." Ross's eyes were not on the lake at all. Dorie found him staring at her. "And I think the view from where I'm sitting is the best."

"You have me now. You don't have to say all those sweet things anymore."

Ross tilted his head. "I know, but they're still true."

Dorie relinquished her spot at the window and claimed a seat next to him. Ross put his arms around her.

"See? This is the best spot on the boat." Ross kissed her and held her close.

Dorie had to agree.

A lady near them smiled. "Newlyweds?"

"Yes, ma'am. Does it show?"

She nodded, and her smile widened. "Don't ever forget to enjoy each other. I was married fifty-five years before my Harold died. What I would give for a snuggle with him." Her eyes misted over. She dug through her purse for a tissue.

A younger version of the lady sat beside her and put her arm around here. "Are you okay, Mum?"

193

"Of course, just missing your da." She dabbed her eyes with the tissue. "Don't make a fuss. I'm fine."

Soon they were docking without having seen the fabled Nessie.

Then they were all trundled onto the tour bus again. The bus headed through the Great Glen to Ben Nevis, the tallest mountain in the UK, after which they stopped for coffee and refreshments.

Back on the bus they went to Glen Coe and Rannoch Moor (the film home of James Bond in the movie Skyfall). By 3:30, the sun had disappeared. Before heading back to Edinburgh, the bus drove through Stirling and past the great castle. In the distance, Dorie spied the William Wallace monument, bringing to mind the movie Braveheart.

By the time they returned to Edinburgh, it was 8:30. Dorie and Ross headed down the hill to the Grassmarket and fell into bed.

On the 28th, Dorie and Ross visited Edinburgh Castle and shopped the Christmas markets and small shops down the Royal Mile. They bought souvenirs for Riley, Angela, and Dorie's family. They found booklets on Clan Ross, tartan ties, wool scarves, plaid blankets, and the Ross clan crest brooch. Ross bought Dorie a Celtic cross necklace. They picked out a Christmas ornament for their tree.

Dorie and Ross found the Greyfriars Bobby, a Skye terrier monument, and rubbed his nose. The Skye terrier Bobby spent the remaining days of his life next to the grave of his policeman owner, John Grey, at the Greyfriars Cemetery. The people of Edinburgh fed the dog for fourteen years while he remained beside the grave. When he died, he was buried near his master.

They bought a new suitcase in which to carry their purchases home.

On the 29th, a tour bus took them to Rosslyn Chapel, the climactic end of Dan Brown's book, The Da Vinci Code, the Borders with Hadrian's Wall, the town of Melrose, and the ruins of Melrose Abbey, where the heart of Robert the Bruce is fabled to be buried.

By the 30th, the Hogmanay festival activities began. Hogmanay is the celebration of the last day of the year.

After passing the Walker Slater Menswear store every day on the curved Victoria Street, Dorie finally convinced Ross to buy a new suit. The store was full of suits in various plaids and tweeds.

"You know it's hard to fit me in a regular suit." Ross browsed the pants, finally finding his size in a plaid he enjoyed. "If they fit, I'll buy them. We don't have time to have them altered."

The store clerk stepped up to direct Ross to the dressing room. "We are happy to ship to America, sir."

While he was changing, Dorie and the clerk looked for a vest and suit coat to match the brown plum windowpane lambswool plaid Ross had chosen. Guessing at Ross's size, the clerk took them into the bowels of the dressing room.

Ross appeared wearing the pants. "I can't believe it. These actually fit, though they need to be hemmed."

"We can have them hemmed for you by

tomorrow." The clerk brushed past looking for the next size up to accommodate Ross's strong arms and shoulders.

The clerk brought him another vest and William jacket. He slipped them on with his long sleeve t-shirt.

"Oh my." Dorie sank into a chair.

"Do you like it?" Ross did a little model walk and pose.

"It's lovely, Ross. The coloring is perfect with your sandy hair and coppery beard."

The clerk examined the fit. "It's perfect."

Ross shook his head. "And right off the rack."

The clerk ran off for pins and measuring tape to hem the pants.

"Should we really spend this much money on a suit right now? It's not cheap."

Dorie looked at him. "It looks so good on you. It fits. It's good quality. Yes, you should buy it."

"Okay. Just don't throw anymore coffee on me while I'm wearing it."

They both laughed. The clerk looked uncertain about the reason for their laughter.

Ross took another look in the mirror. "I'll take it."

"Very good. Let me measure the hem, and the pants will be done by tomorrow."

After another day on the town, Ross and Dorie joined the torchlight procession from Edinburgh Castle to Holyrood Palace, watched fireworks, and danced in the streets with an inestimable crowd of Scots and tourists.

The 30th blended into the 31st, with more festival

activities well into the night. At the chiming of midnight at New Years, the entire crowd sang Auld Lang Syne. Dorie and Ross fell into bed knowing they were flying home on the 2nd.

DIANE E. TATUM

About the Author

www.dianeetatumwriter.com
tatumlight@gmail.com

Diane E. Tatum began writing in grade school with short mystery stories, a play performed by her sixth-grade class, and a dictionary of supernatural beings. High school found her writing serial fiction with her friends, including developing characters and plot lines through hand-written notes.

Her first book, Gold Earrings, is an outgrowth of a short story written in a high school creative writing class. She is writing a historical Christian series called Colonial Dream. The first novel is A Time to Fight, the second is A Time to Love, and the third is

A Time to Choose. She has also written a series of mysteries called Mainstreet Mysteries: #1 Kudzu Sculptures, #2 Gemini Conspiracy, and #3 Attic Visitations.

In addition to her writing career, Diane taught middle school language arts for 11 years. She has worked as a church youth group leader and worker since 1981. She currently serves as an adjunct professor of English at Motlow State Community College.

She is loved and supported by her husband, Ken, and their two sons and daughters-in-law. Their four young grandsons are a joy to them all.

Books by Diane E. Tatum
Gold Earrings
Mission Mesquite
Oxford Fairy Tale
Colonial Dream, Book 1: A Time to Fight
Colonial Dream, Book 2: A Time to Love
Colonial Dream, Book 3: A Time to Choose
Main Street Mysteries: Kudzu Sculptures
Main Street Mysteries #2: The Gemini Conspiracy
Main Street Mysteries #3: Attic Visitations

Coming soon!
Colonial Dream, Book 4: A Time to Create
MISStletoe Romances: Dreaming of a Wedded Christmas
Mainstreet Mysteries #4:

Bible Study Questions for Attic Visitations, Main Street Mysteries #3

Several themes run through this story: What happened with Ross's mom? The impact a trauma can have on those who experience it. The jealousy of Emmie. The importance of marriage. The resistance of sexual impurity before and after marriage.

The birthday party:

Read these verses: Leviticus 19:14-18; John 7:24; James 5:8-9; Zechariah 8:17; Romans 12:10, 13:8; 2 Corinthians 13:11; Galatians 5:13; Ephesians 4:2; 1 Thessalonians 3:12, 4:9; 2 Thessalonians 1:3; Hebrews 10:24; 1 Peter 4:4-11; 1 John 3:11-24, 4:4-21; Matthew 5:32-48.

1)   Jeanine MacAvoy murdered three adults at the party, but she also destroys the innocence of the children at the birthday party.

a. How do we deal with senseless acts of violence?

b. How do we 'judge' someone who has clearly lost a sense of right and wrong?

c. How do we help victims of violence survive?

2)   Sally says she had an affair with Glen MacAvoy, and that caused the attacks.

a. Can we take her word as truth? Why/Why not?

b. If it's true, is Ross's father responsible for what happened?

c. If it's not true, is there any way to prove it? How would you write it?

3) Children were witnesses to the crime at the party.

a. How do adults help children process the act of violence?

b. How does the legal system care for its crime victims?

4) In this story, I wrote that Emmie responded to betrayal the same way Jeanine MacAvoy did. Does that seem appropriate given the trauma in her past?

5) Considering the stigma mental illness has had in the past, how should Christians respond to persons suffering from depression to psychosis? How would God want Christians to respond? What is the church's responsibility?

The purity of marriage:

Read these verses: Mark 7:14-23; Galatians 5:13-26; Ephesians 5:15-33; 1 Corinthians 7:1-9; 2 Corinthians 6:1-6; 1 Thessalonians 4:1-8.

1) Ross and Dorie struggle with attraction prior to marriage, which is normal.

a. What ways should Christians deal with desire prior to marriage?

b. Is it different when they experience desire outside their marriage?

c. The world outside the church struggles with the reason sexual purity is necessary. How would you explain it to a non-Christian?

2) Sex is not the only reason for marriage. What else is important in a marriage?

What other ways of being intimate might occur in a marriage?

3) If Glen MacAvoy was unfaithful to Jeanine, in what ways did that compromise their family? While her reaction is extreme, how does unfaithfulness destroy a relationship and a family?

4) God allows divorce in the Mosaic law for cases of unfaithfulness. Think about Joseph wanting to deal honorably with Mary (not have her stoned or scandalized) when she became pregnant with Jesus. What ideals does Joseph model for 21st century Christians?

5) What advice would you give to young (or old!) newlyweds? What Bible verse might you give them?

6) How important is Riley's promise to respect Ross's marriage to Dorie, especially if she begins working at Daelin PD?

DIANE E. TATUM

Chapter 1 of Main Street Mysteries #4

Chapter 1
Getting Ross and Dorie home …

Riley stood in Atlanta Hartsfield Airport waiting for Ross and Dorie's flight to land from their honeymoon in Scotland. He had taken them to the airport on Christmas day following their wedding on the twenty-fourth.

"Look over here. I bet this is their flight!" Jenny had come with him. She was staring out the window, waiting for planes to land. "Riley, come look and tell me if I'm right."

Riley sauntered over to where Jenny and her ponytail twitched with excitement. He slipped his arms around her, timidly at first then with growing confidence. They had been dating just since the wedding. A whole week. It seemed to Riley it had been longer than that. Of course, he'd known her longer from his regular stops at the Corner Café diner where she waited tables. Then she turned up cooking and waiting on guests at Ross and Dorie's wedding a week ago. They'd been together ever since.

Of course, his best friends had been in Scotland. Now the plane was late, and they'd still have the drive to Helen after Ross and Dorie deplaned, went through luggage retrieval, Customs, and Border Control. Maybe it had not been a good idea to bring Jenny along.

"American is pleased to announce the arrival of Flight 36 from Edinburgh, Scotland."

"Thank God." Riley was feeling impatient and

unsure, two things he hated to feel. He'd rather be in control of a situation.

"They're here!" Jenny ran to the gateway from the secure terminal area.

"It's still going to be a while before they come out. Why don't we get coffee?" Riley steered her toward a Starbucks Coffeeshop. "We can get a pastry or a sandwich or something."

"Aren't you excited to see them?" Jenny walked backwards while talking to Riley. "They could have cool souvenirs. And they've been married, you know, able to sleep together for a week."

"And there's something I will not be asking about when they arrive." Riley chuckled and steered Jenny to walking forward to avoid the oncoming crowds. Riley's phone chimed, indicating a text message. "Ross says they are at the gate and preparing to get off the plane. He'll keep me informed."

Jenny probably didn't need a cup of coffee. She was bouncing while she walked. Would she crash on the way home, or rev up even more? Hard to tell. This relationship was still so new.

"Hurry, Riley, we don't want to miss them."

"They can't get home without us."

The line was long, but there was plenty of time. Once they ordered and received their coffee and food, Riley guided Jenny to a bistro table in the walkway.

"I've been meaning to ask where you go to church. I'd be happy to go with you or you can go with me." A bite of iced pound cake gave Jenny a chance to speak.

"Hmmm. Well, I really don't go to church regularly." Jenny sipped her coffee. "Is that a problem, Riley?"

Riley took a deep breath. "It depends. Are you a Christian?"

"Sure, I'm an American living in the Bible Belt." Jenny peeled the paper from the muffin she'd chosen. "My mom and dad didn't take me to church. After their car accident, I moved in with my Aunt Flo who runs the Doll House B&B in Helen. Sunday mornings are premium for cleaning with guests coming and going."

Riley's heart sank. *Do not be yoked to an unbeliever.*

Riley's phone chimed again. "They have their luggage and are headed for Customs and Border Control." He drank a long sip of his espresso to avoid talking about Christ with Jenny. That would need to wait for a day that she was open to listen. Or not at all, but he guessed he had a responsibility to at least share his faith before the relationship became too serious.

***

Dorie was glad to be on Georgia soil once again, but thoroughly exhausted by the nine-hour return flight. Ross had the two bags they had taken, and she rolled the new bag nearly bursting with souvenirs, gifts, and Ross's new wool suit.

They approached the official US border agent's booth together. He looked at them both and at their passports.

"You just came from Scotland?"

"Yes, sir. It was our honeymoon." Dorie was so

excited to be Ross's wife. She'd been telling nearly everyone they had met on this trip.

"Your passport is in your maiden name then?"

"Yes, sir. Is that a problem?" A glance at Ross, and she knew he was embarrassed. Flames of blush painted his throat and face.

"Do you have another form of ID with you, ma'am?"

Dorie dug in her purse and produced her driver's license.

"Where do you live now? Is either of these addresses correct?"

That's when Dorie had an inkling of fear. "No, sir. I live at Ross's house. The address on his passport."

The agent checked Ross's passport. "Get those documents updated, Mrs. MacAvoy."

"Yes, sir."

He stamped both their passports. "Welcome home to the United States of America. Congratulations on your marriage." He then grinned a toothy smile.

Ross roared with laughter. "Thank you."

Dorie felt confused and a little angry. Ross pulled her through the aisle and into the terminal.

"He was just giving you a hard time." Ross laughed again.

Dorie drug her luggage behind her. "How was I to know to update my passport and my license, so they at least had the same address? I didn't know we were going international for our honeymoon."

"No, you did not. That's what makes it a surprise, y'know?" Ross walked backwards and gave her a smile.

Dorie stopped and sat on her bag.

Ross stopped and rolled his luggage up to her. "Let's go home to our own bed."

She crossed her arms. "I don't think I can move another step."

"Ah, darling, you're just being stubborn now. Come on. Riley and Jenny are waiting to drive us home." He wrapped his arms around her. "I love you."

"Okay, but I am so tired. You may end up carrying me."

A porter approached them. "Do you need help with your luggage?"

"Apparently we do." Ross picked Dorie up. "I've got my wife. Can you get the three bags?"

The porter smiled. "Yes, sir."

People in the terminal began clapping and cheering.

Dorie threw her arms around Ross's neck. "What are you doing? You're embarrassing me."

"No, darling, I'm taking you home." Ross held her close. "There's Riley, and Jenny?"

"You can put me down, Ross." Dorie faced forward and saw Riley and, yes, Jenny from the B&B.

"Once we're out of the secure area, I'll put you down. If you want me to, I'll carry you all the way to the car. I only want what's good for you." Ross held her close. "I know you're tired. I am, too. Let's just go home."

Dorie and Ross followed Riley and Jenny to the parking garage. The porter took the bags all the way to the car. They threw the bags in the back, then climbed in.

Riley started the car. "Next stop, Helen, Georgia."